DEATH AND DOUBLING CUBES

A 10,000 DAWNS TALE

BY JAMES WYLDER

ILLUSTRATED BY RACHEL JOHNSON

Edited by Gwen Ragno.

ISBN:1547082852
ISBN-13:978-1547082858

DEDICATION

To Jo,
My Bestest Pal,
My closest Comrade.

Rebel Rebel,
You'd tear up anything.

FILE REGISTRY

ACKNOWLEDGMENTS

I wrote the first draft of this book in 2012. The road to getting it released over the last five years has been long and difficult. This book wouldn't have been possible without so many people that its not even worth mentioning them all. Oh well, I'll try. I'll probably miss many of you. So thank you to:
Rachel Johnson, Gwen Ragno, David Koon, Jo Smiley, Taylor Elliott, Jordan Stout, Miguel Ramirez, Brandon Derk, Elizabeth Tock, Emmeryn Hempstead. Ellie Fairfield, Gara Gaines, Keegan Mixdorf, Baylor Dowdy, Luke Lentz, Rusty Blaker, Colby McClung, Olivia Hinkel, John Harbaugh, Joshua Anderson, Rebecca Jacob, Maria Grosso, Jim Perry, Nathan P. Butler, Sean E. Williams, Aaron Copeasetik, Kathy Barbour, Josh Radke, Kassandra Radke, Kala Grae, Katie Green, Jon Becraft, RJ Sullivan, Kylie Leane, the Hanover College Coffee Shop, Kaffine Coffee, the Electric Brew Elkhart, and the IUPUI University Library, Rob, Martha, and Molly Southgate, Evan Forman, Michael Robertson, Ashley Sims-Cleaveland, Brandi Hornbuckle, John Cleaveland, Corey Roth, Damon Null, David Blockzynski, Andrea Ramirez, and probably many more.

Thank you all.

TOP

SECRET

FOR THE LIBRARIAN'S EYES ONLY

Reading this document without the proper clearance is considered an act of treason to the Index. If you aren't a member of the Index and you read this, well...don't.

To: The Librarian
From: Carl Fredrickson
Subject: My previous manuscript
Timestamp: 5:24 GMT Earthtime

Chess Mistress Hex,

You didn't need to have Ryan slam me against the wall to tell me you weren't happy with my report. While I can understand your desire to "be able to read this without falling asleep," in the future I would prefer if I was given advance notice to try to make my catalog of events entertaining, rather than well cited. I'm not particularly proficient at prose, but being that it seems like you would prefer this document rewritten as creative non-fiction since you underlined and circled the words "creative non-fiction," which appear to be written in human blood at the top of the returned document, I shall oblige. You are, after all, infinitely wise and entirely in control of my paycheck.

Also, that you actually did fall asleep reading the document is entirely my fault. In the colloquial: my bad.

If my chronicle of these events is to be readable, we have to go back to the events which preceded them. We can't simply jump straight into the infiltration of battle fleets, the strange life of Jhe Aladdin, or the saga of the Hypercube family in these dark times without understanding the actually still pretty darn dark times they originated from.

A long time ago, Jhe Sang Ki — better known by his professional Snowcutter handle Kalingkata (Snowcutter being the term for the Rimward's unofficial hacker/infiltrators) — and his frenemy Chess Mistress Hex, aka you, shoved their fellow Snowcutter Backgammon Kate off of a catwalk to her very timely death. This story also begins after you, Chess Mistress Hex, killed some guy called the Librarian and took over his criminal empire. Slinking in like a very elegant tiger. Then everyone banded together and beat back Invaders from taking over Mars, and things were good. Mostly good, at least. Kalingkata married his long-suffering sweetheart Hotaru Kowano and they had five children, including their youngest, whom Sang Ki named Aladdin (much to his wife's chagrin, but it was a comprimise to naming the kid Ziggy). You were war heroes, and there was peace. You left a legacy.

But things got bad. You'd fought a war, but then we met the horror we call the Council and their Three Emperors, and it turned out that what we thought was the war was really just the first shot of a much biggest interuniversal conflict the likes of which I still have trouble comprehending. The Council decided their own multi-universe empire wasn't big enough, looked at ours, and thought, "Hey, let's have a go at that, shall we?" They hopped over with an army to take over our pretty little solar system. That was kind of a bad day, and a bad day that the children of the heroes of the last war had to deal with, including Jhe Aladdin.

This story is about Aladdin, but it's also about Kalingkata's personal assistant, Backgammon Jenny, and it's really not worth telling you the story without telling you about her.

This took a lot of work, so please consider giving me a

raise upon completion of your reading.

Best Regards,

Carl Fredrickson

Carl Fredrickson

FILE 1:
FAMILY REUNION

For a moment, he was on the computer and in a war zone, and his hands clenched up, but they relaxed as Hotaru leaned her head on Sang Ki's shoulder. He was typing, which was practically like saying "Sang Ki was in the room." His eyes darted in every direction, and windows popped up and down on the screen. They sat together in silence for a few moments as his pulse slowed, and his fingers began moving at their normal rapid pace.

"What are you typing honey?" She said, running her fingers through his short hair.

"Er, let's see, I'm re-coding Mars' oxygen factory AIs, since I convinced Natsu I could get them to run more efficiently, and I'm reading up on Citlal biology, and writing an essay for the Ryuu Post-Gazette about the work Fei and I have been doing."

"You could just do one thing at a time."

"Not when I'm writing an essay. I hate writing essays."

"How far are you?"

His face went funny. "Almost done, I just can't end it."

Hotaru nuzzled into the groove in his neck. "Well I'm done for the day, and Aladdin is off with his friends, so you can show it to me if you want."

He smiled. "Absolutely. Though I've been thinking about how Aladdin is getting older. When I was 16, I signed up for the military. When I was seventeen, I fought a war..." He trailed off for a moment, trying not to go back to the battlefield. "He's our youngest, but he's still going to grow up. I can't help but worry he's going to have to go through hell too."

She hadn't really thought about that. And she didn't really have an answer, so they bathed in the light of the monitor again for a few minutes.

"Sorry," Sang Ki was the master of awkwardly moving on from topics. "So, want to read it?"

Hotaru smiled, and turned the monitor towards her.

Human Life at the End of the 25th Century
By Jhe Sang Ki

People have been dying for a long time and, since the industrial revolution, at around the same age. There have been a few leaps since then, but generally people assume we have hit the border of how far we can extend human life while that life can still be actively, rather than passively, lived. However, from the last two decades of work I did along with Dr. Tam Fei-Yen, and Doctor Snake—

"Doctor Snake? Seriously?"

"Just read the essay."

—as well as Aequitas of the Citlal, I have come to believe the limits of human life may be extended beyond what we previously dreamed. While this does not mean immortality – and in fact a very strong argument can be made that immortality is immoral due to the limited resources we have access to as a species – it may mean that the high end of 150 would be underestimating things.

"How would we do that?"

"You could read the rest of the essay."

"Its seventy pages long."

"Is it? I guess it will be a serial piece..."

"How, Sang Ki?"

"Well, by using techniques to rejuvenate parts of the body we thought unrepairable without damage to one's own self, like the brain, using some medicine we got from the Citlal, and some discoveries we made by ourselves based on it. Through my work with the Citlal, we have been able to preserve the consciousness of a deceased human for years. After all, if you lose your memories, you're losing the very experience of your own life. To give that back, to save it, would be a miracle. Of course, the ultimate end could be to transfer a person's memories into a new body, which would be immortality."

"That's exciting."

"I certainly hope it is. I don't want to live forever, and I don't want to outlive everyone I know, especially you, but if everyone lives longer, I'm fine with that."

"That sounds exactly like you."

"Well I'd certainly hope so."

* * * * *

Tam Fei-Yen was a Doctor. Not just a small time doctor anymore, but a huge one. At least that's what the council on medicine was saying—and the Nobel committee. Even her old boss, former Chief Surgeon Natsu Mashima, was impressed with her, and he was President of Mars these days.

"Congratulations to you and Sang Ki," Natsu said, sipping his champagne.

"Why thank you President Natsu,"

"Please just call me Natsu."

"Are you serious?"

"No. Always say President."

"Natsu!" Kalingkata sauntered over and slapped him on the shoulder, tipping a bit of his champagne onto the carpet. Natsu's bodyguards didn't look pleased, but this wasn't the first time.

"Ah, Kalingkata. I was just congratulating Fei and you on the awards for your work on gene therapy. A Nobel and a medical council award in the same year? I can't help but be jealous. Or I would be—"

"If you hadn't already won both. We know, Natsu."

"Ridiculous. I'm just proud of my protégé, and my friend."

Sang Ki looked across the room, where Hotaru had apparently talked someone into yet another multi-year business contract. He couldn't help grinning. When she was happy, he was ecstatic. Sang Ki took a sip of his champagne. Cheers to you Hotaru.

"Kalingkata, let me introduce you to a couple here I've worked out a new shipping deal with from Olympia, Geraldine and Michelangelo Hypercube." The champagne didn't fly out so much as sloppily glob down Sang Ki's tuxedo as he turned around.

Beside Natsu were a man and a woman. The man was tall and muscular, like some sort of Grecian statue, every part of him perfectly sculpted by nature. His blue eyes twinkled with inborn warmth, his long blonde hair flowed with enviable grace. If not for the twisted scar marring his left cheek, no one could argue he was the most beautiful man they had ever seen. There was a reason he was named Michelangelo.

The woman looked more like a Rimward. Her entire right arm, leg, and eye had been replaced with mechanical ones. Her brown hair was straight, but mousier then her husband's. Her eyes locked with Sang Ki's. Her metal hand crushed her champagne glass. Some other people talked, but their words were just garbled.

"JackBox."

"Kalingkata."

"Hey."

"Indeed."

"How've you been?"

"Thirteen kids."

"I expected that."

"Fourteen if you count one he had before we met."

"Oh. Still sounds about right."

"You?"

"Five."

"So are you going to introduce us?" Michelangelo spoke.

"Oh, sorry," Geraldine snapped into reality, "Michelangelo, this is my ex-boyfriend Kalingkata."

"Fei, Natsu, this is my ex-girlfriend JackBox."

There are some moments in life that are just so awkward no one really knows what to say, but no one can break out of the moment to leave it. Instead, the people involved resign themselves to that fate and hope for someone to break the strain of awkward.

"Sang Ki! I landed a deal with DroTech."

"Congrats sweetie."

Hotaru looked at the awkward states. "Who are these guys?"

"They're, uh..."

Fei cut in. "Hotaru, Sang Ki has told you about Geraldine Hypercube before right?"

He had.

"Oh, well nice to meet you." Hands were shaken.

"So, Sang Ki end up a good dad?"

Hotaru poked Sang Ki in the side. "Of course he did."

Geraldine nodded and looked down at her feet."So, any of your kids here?"

Hotaru looked at Geraldine's feet, too. She could see the gizmos working in the right one."Yes, Aladdin is here, and Kotone, and Jari, and the twins...actually, that's all of the kids. All of the kids are here."

"I'd love to meet them."

Michelangelo chimed in. "Some of our kids are here, not all of them. It's hard to get them all in one place."

Fei and Natsu exchanged a glance, wondering if they should back out of the conversation.

"Actually, I think they headed out early."

"I just saw Anya and Ulysses—"

"No, they headed out. And I think we should, too. It was a pleasure meeting you, Jhe Hotaru, and seeing you again Kalingkata. We'll talk again soon Natsu." She turned to Fei, "Sorry we didn't really get to chat, Doctor." She grabbed her ridiculously attractive husband by the arm and tugged him away from the group.

Natsu thought, and thought he shouldn't say it, but really, he couldn't resist.

"Kalingkata, you had a Rimward robot girlfriend who's now married to Michelangelo with fourteen kids?"

"Yes, yes I did."

"I didn't even know you had a girlfriend before Hotaru!"

"Natsu, shut up," Sang Ki muttered.

"Shut up, Natsu," Fei grumbled.

Hotaru just punched him. The body guards didn't even flinch. It wasn't the first time.

Hotaru, Sang Ki, Natsu, Fei, their spouses and all of their children went out to dinner that night. It was good to see everyone together, the kids chatting, a few of them clearly interested in dating now that they were old enough.

Aequitas came by, though he had trouble fitting through the doorframe due to his large form and the food wasn't much to his liking. After a few serious words with Sang Ki and Natsu, he seemed to have fun playing with the younger kids, and for a moment the gathering felt like an extended family.

They wouldn't be together like this again for years. Maybe ever. Mars floated in its orbit, and on its back rode their smiles.

Aequitas didn't stay long, despite several of them trying to convince him to stick around, and soon the party became smaller clumps, huddled at tables or standing in trios. Sang Ki, Hotaru, and Natsu were laughing about something when Sang Ki stopped and stared into his glass.

"Something wrong, Kalingkata?"

"No, nothing."

Natsu didn't ask further and, seeing his daughter Lalita trying to sneak behind the bar, stormed off to wag his finger at her. As soon as he left, Hotaru lowered her eyebrows and asked the same question.

"Is something wrong?"

"Yeah, I just...I hadn't seen her in decades, since she got kicked off Mars. I was happy to see her, but it seemed like there was something she wasn't telling me."

"People change. It was probably hard for her to see you."

Sang Ki shrugged. "Nothing for her to hold back. Thirteen kids with Michelangelo, and me married to the best woman ever born? It would have been fine if she'd just stuck around longer."

Hotaru smiled. "World keeps turning."

"Let's go to talk to the others. You don't live forever, you know."

"And you can't know everything."

"That's what you think." They chuckled and walked over to their laughing friends, the laughs vanishing the higher they went, till all there was, was space.

For all the stars in the Universe, only one had Earth, Mars, and Titan orbiting it. Long ago they had just been blips in telescopes, and now they were large colored marbles that passed by Geraldine's eyes.

"You didn't tell him," Michelangelo said. Geraldine could hear the disapproval in his voice.

"He's got his own life now, Michelangelo. Him and that Hotaru woman go well together. He looked happier with her then he ever did with me. It's better to just leave the past in the past. Not dredge it up. He'll never know. Frankly, that's best for everyone."

"Not know what?" Anya and Ulysses came in, followed by Zoroaster and Cleopatra. There were ten other Hypercube children. She'd made quite the family with Michelangelo.

"Nothing, Ulysses."

Out of all twelve of the kids, Anya and Ulysses were the only two who looked markedly different. Anya was brilliantly blonde with an air of old Russia about her, and Ulysses had black hair and looked more Korean.

Geraldine remembered when Michelangelo and she got married. She was still JackBox then, a renegade ne'er-do-well. Five months pregnant with another man's baby, but Michelangelo didn't care. He had a newborn daughter from that Index whore. Or at least Geraldine liked to think of her that way. I certainly wouldn't say that about someone.

She always thought Michelangelo and Kalingkata would have gotten along great – Jhes and Hypercubes as the best of friends – but she knew that couldn't be.

Things could only get more awkward.

"Ulysses, Anya, you love your mommy, right?"

They looked at each other. That question came out of nowhere. "Of course, mom."

"Never visit the Spinneret on Ceres. Promise?"

"Promise."

"Promise."

"Good," Geraldine leaned against the windows and watched the passing stars. She was older than she had been. She could still close her eyes and see Kalingkata, 20-some years younger, without a wrinkle or grey hair, laughing as she made terrible puns for him in their apartment over breakfast. She held her spoon with her metal hand. Her real fingertips touched his.

That was all gone, though, and Michelangelo had been a better husband and father than she could have dreamed. But in a lot of ways, Kalingkata never left.

And the ship slipped through the darkness toward Olympus Station above Titan, a tiny blip on the whole of reality, swallowed up amidst the entirety of their lives.

Research Sketch:
Jhe "Kalingkata" Sang Ki

Profile:

-Veteran of the Martian Revolution as a young man.

-Married to Vacuum Cleaner heiress Hotaru Kowano.

-Pop Culture Junkie.

-Expert Hacker.

-Part of the notorious "Hand of Glycon" crew that reshaped the political landscape 20 years ago.

-Has chronic depression and PTSD, but has had plenty of treatment.

Carl Fredrickson

FILE 2:
BACKGAMMON KATE:
THE NEXT GENERATION

Kalingkata stepped into the elevator, and held up his hand to give the guard a high five. The guard stood stoically. Kalingkata held the pose for about a minute.

"I'm wearing you down, Xi Greg." He relaxed as his companion stepped into the elevator.

"He's never going to, sir," his companion said, as she stared at the elevator doors.

"How would you know? Do you know Greg? Have you ever gone down to the Rimward Accord Meeting Chambers before?"

He had her there. "No."

"Exactly," Kalingkata looked at the wall. He figured out the exact speed the elevator was moving, judging by the disturbance of particles caused by the g-dampeners. It was faster than usual.

"Shouldn't we be working? Why are we seeing an AI, even a planetary one, right now?"

"I haven't stopped working."

He hadn't. Other men's minds withered with time. Kalingkata's had blossomed. As they stood there, he continued running the calculations he'd been working for exactly how temporary states of reality were pulled through into our own, and somehow manipulated. The numbers were quite possibly the most complex thing anyone had ever tried to calculate, and Kalingkata loved it; he hadn't been challenged like that in years. And yet, he thought, the challenge was better while he was talking. That was the real secret to why he never shut up.

"Hey, Greg, did I ever tell you the story of how I met my assistant here?"

Greg stared stoically at the elevator doors.

"Great! Then it will be new to you. It's an adventure, and it involves me and the Chess Mistress killing someone, and meeting her afterwards. It's great fun."

"Not this again."

"So, it all started when..."

* * * * *

Sang Ki watched Aladdin kick his heels against the swivelly chair he was sitting in aboard the "Spider from Mars," his flagship. He wondered if you could really call three old Martian battleships, a few repurposed Centro cruisers from Earth, a clone of the ridiculously named flagship of the Index: "The Hand of Glycon," and all the various tiny ships the Spinneret usually had a "fleet," but he didn't say that out loud. Pretend he was important. Fake it till you make it. At least keep up appearances so when he went out for kebabs with you he could tell you that he had a fleet and then stick his tongue out, as he was technically right.

Aladdin's mother Hotaru was nearby, reading a book to Aladdin, "The Once and Future King," about King Arthur and his knights. She looked up to check up on Sang Ki's Prep work.

"Did you pack your grenades, honey?"

"I don't really think I'll need them."

"Sang Ki. Come on. When would bringing grenades hurt?"

"A volcano?"

"Be serious."

"You're right. As usual." Sang Ki chucked some grenades into a satchel, and leaned over to kiss Hotaru. Aladdin squirmed in his seat. He was clearly going through that "kissing is weird" phase of childhood. Sang Ki walked over and tousled his hair, "I'll see you in a little bit little Jhe."

"Are you seeing Hexie, Daddy?"

"Yep, only we won't be eating kebabs today."

"What will you be eating?"

He paused. "Victory," he said, in a way that made it impossible to tell if he was joking or completely serious. Hotaru let out a sigh as he said it, rolling her eyes politely. That answer clearly puzzled Aladdin, but Sang Ki left him with it as he affixed his helmet and headed to the airlock.

It was time to do something stupid, and Kalingkata couldn't wait. Stupidity was the only thing that broke up the monotony of knowing everything. As the airlock sealed itself and the ship rotated into the correct position around Europa, he took a deep breath, then realized it really wasn't necessary since he was in a space suit and was going to be dropping from orbit in a moment.

"You could just take a shuttle, sir," the airlock attendant noted.

"Shut up!"

"Really, it wouldn't be an inconvenience..."

"SHUT UP! I'm jumping from a spaceship. It gives me the element of surpr—"

The hatch opened, and the air and a single body vented from the port into the blackness of space, which soon became the thin atmosphere of Europa.

Sang Ki's limbs flailed for a moment, the edges of his suit looked almost on fire and the ground started to look very large. Then, he moved his body into position with his chest down, his arms like wings, and seemed to flutter down like a lead-lined feather onto a solid metal dome. The suit dampened the impact to nearly nothing and the magnets in his shoes and gloves stuck him to it like a fly—a panting, sweating fly.

"That was a terrible idea," he muttered, clanking his way to an entry hatch. He hacked it open and dropped in with a seamlessness not expected of a man who had just fallen straight from orbit onto a metal ball.

The drop was actually more uncomfortable than the one from space, as the suit was only programmed to dampen the effects of long falls, and Kalingkata's legs ached a bit. He got up and began staggering. There wasn't any time to waste, after all. You could get yourself killed, and then he wouldn't have anyone to play chess with.

The alarms were naturally silent, and Kalingkata needed to find the intruder—the one you hadn't seen coming. He was so going to be giving you shit about this for years. Kalingkata threw his helmet off and let it clatter along the floor.

"Kalingkata!"your voice yelled over the intercom. "Are you in here?"

"Yeah, I'm here. I bet you'd rather be elsewhere,

though."

"The doors are jammed!"

"Did you try hacking them?"

"Shut up, Mr. Jhe."

"Shut up, Miss—" a hissing sound came over the intercom.

"I think she's venting the room."

"I'll be there soon."

"Don't slant rhyme at me!"

"It's fine."

Kalingkata ran a whole 12 feet to the nearest wall terminal and got into the system. The Hacker had been clever and waited till you were in a room without wall terminals, for security reasons, before jamming all the doors in the base.

"Clever girl," he muttered, as though there was a dinosaur nearby.

She was good, but she was no Kalingkata. He shut off the venting. He opened the magnetic locks on the doors. Unfortunately, she'd shifted the power from the track rails that moved the doors, and they'd all have to be opened manually. Fun. From the looks of it, most of the base had been gassed...non-lethally. He noted that. This girl was good.

You were still trying to pry the door open when Kalingkata reached you. I mean, I'm sure you would have been fine if he hadn't, but the the door was being tricky. Luckily, Kalingkata had a crowbar. Unluckily, he wasn't any stronger than you. The two of you slowly forced the door open, straining your muscles, your brow forming beads of sweat your impeccable face rarely showed.

"I have my own crowbar, you know," you said.

"Well then you should have brought it."

"It's mounted! It's a historic artifact!"

The door was open enough for you to slide through, and you did, the metal doors popping buttons and ripping bits away from your extremely expensive clothes as you squeezed through. You looked a bit awful, which only made me sympathize with you more in your dire situation. There clearly hadn't been much air in the room.

"We need to move. You can tell me about the historic crowbar later," Kalingkata said.

You nodded and, with a hand on Kalingkata's shoulder to support yourself, started walking. You got about three steps before Kalingkata halted, and you looked up to see a young lady with light brown skin in a red and green plaid poodle skirt, knee-high socks and a black turtleneck shirt, with her dark brown hair in a ponytail and a gun in her hand.

"Chess Mistress Hex and Kalingkata. The Index and the Spinneret all in one basket." She spit her words out like she was addressing the prince and princess of hell. "I've been waiting a long time to meet you two. And finish the job my mother started."

You raised an eyebrow. So did Kalingkata. In a moment like that, a person only has two choices. 1. Ask the person to explain the thing hanging over the conversation that they all assumed everyone was aware of, but were just uncertain enough of to not want to make things even more awkward than the gun was making it. 2. Just awkwardly blurt it out. I suppose they could also run away, or talk about eggs, but that would just be silly.

"Backgammon Kate reproduced? She had sex? With a human?"you blurted out.

"My mother was a better woman than you'll ever be!"

"It's uncouth to compare people you've never met, dear."

The girl almost fired, but Kalingkata raised a hand. "Now there, what's your name?"

"Backgammon Jenny, you son of a bitch. And don't you forget me."

"I don't usually forget poodle skirts, though I would if you shot me in the head."

He stepped closer, "Now, why don't we deal with this like civilized folk? You clearly are a telepath."

"No I'm not."

"Yes you are."

"No I'm not!"

"Yes you are! Bowie in heaven, I tracked you here, how else do you think I did it?"

"I was wondering why you two were in the same place. I thought I'd only get Hex today."

"Convenient, ey?"

"Can you just shoot us both already? I'm getting bored." you said, picking at a loose button. Kalingkata ignored you, keeping a placid look on his face as he replied.

"Now, Jenny, who do you think we are?"

"You're the people who killed my mom!"

"Yes, we are that. I'll admit we did both shove her—"

"—to her brutal demise. Gory, even."

"...Yes, Hexie."

Jenny shook her head.

"But you're more than that, which makes what you did even more...foul."

"What are we?

"You are...my fathers!"

There is only one option in this situation, and

Kalingkata and you found that you had to follow it to the letter. You looked at each other and slowly started giggling, then fell to the floor laughing incessantly.

"It's...it's not funny!"

"Why...why in space would you think that?" you stammered, wiping tears from your eyes.

"My mom left me a letter, told me she'd combined your genetics into—"

Kalingkata laughed so loud he squeaked, and waved his arm dismissively. Jenny bit her lip so hard it would leave marks, as he took a deep breath and rose to help you up off the floor.

"She did no such thing. Your dad's name was Sam Samson. He worked cleaning grease from ship engines. He died during the Second Rim Wars, after the Martian Revolution, when a ship overheated while he was working on it. Mostly vaporized him."

Her gun lowered an inch.

"How do you know that?"

"Because I've been keeping tabs on you," he said to her calmly, at which you raised an eyebrow, barely. "Because you're right. Hex and I did kill your mom."

The gun went back up.

Kalingkata continued. "So, I have a challenge for you, Jenny. You can talk with people telepathically right? The same rare way people have been able to since Gillen's experiment ripped all those portals into different universes. You're tapped into some alternate reality version of yourself who always could, and you use it well. Not just that, but you're good at it. I'd bet you can even invade people's minds."

"How the hell did you know that?"

"Tabs. Now, try to take over my mind. I know that

implant is how you broke in here. Go on."

Jenny stared into his eyes. She knew he wasn't a fighter or a tactician. He was just some chump who lucked out and was in the right place at the right time with the right people to fill a power vacuum.

"Fine," she yelled, and pushed her consciousness out, lashing at Kalingkata like a rainstorm of whips.

That was when it all disappeared—the base, Hex, Kalingkata, her own body...

Suddenly she was in a strange garden of geometric plants, facing a man – maybe it was a man – who resembled Kalingkata. The features were definitely his, though somewhat less Korean, but the build was more androgynous, more slender. The eyes a bit keener, harsher even, and stripes of blonde rifled his black hair.

Her first instinct was to try to pull out of his mind. She'd been in people's minds before, she'd done it. But it was like someone was holding her mind there gently now, which meant her mind was in a mess of trouble.

"Welcome to my mind, Jenny. I'm afraid I'm a bit too much of an old hand at this for you to really be able to take me over, but at least you can see the waiting room." He picked up a flower with a square bloom. "But more importantly, we're alone. I wanted to talk to you."

"You're Kalingkata? You look..."

"Womany? Rimward-y?"

"Yeah. I thought you were Martian."

"I am, but a while back I spent some time living inside a woman's body due to a freak accident. My mind joined into hers. It's a long story. I kept her memories: living, dying, giving birth... It's strange to hold onto them. But here I am, as I truly am. And so are you."

Jenny felt strangely insecure. "Shut up, I just came

here to kill you."

"And I came to give you something." A blue light appeared in Kalingkata's hands. "I may not have your rather fantastic ability to enter the minds of others, but the woman I was a part of did, and it's given me an uncanny ability to hold it back—a handy side effect of being a woman."

"I still don't really believe you. Joined your memories with someone else? That's impossible. People have tried it before, but it never held, or it went egregiously wrong."

"Then at least believe my gift to you."

Jenny reached out. It felt warm.

"What is it?"

"A memory."

"What do you think this will change?"

"I think you'll accept the job offer I'm about to give you."

She touched it. "Not happening."

She opened her eyes and found herself back in the Index base, you and Kalingkata staring at her. She found herself short of breath, still gasping from the revelation she'd seen. "I'll take the job."

"What job?" you inquired, quirking a brow. . .

And that was how Backgammon Jenny became Sang Ki's personal assistant. As though she hadn't just tried to kill him, he took her up from Europa and onto the bridge of "The Spider From Mars." The whole time she fiddled with a trinket: a hair band with a half-sun, half-moon on it, her life changing so quickly. On the bridge she met Jhe Aladdin, sitting, still swinging his feet, who looked up at her and smiled as Jenny stared around the bridge.

"Well, welcome to the Spider From Mars," Kalingkata said. "Congratulations on falling into my web."

* * * * *

"So that's the story," Kalingkata said as the elevator whirred to a halt. The guard did not look impressed. Jenny was staring at the wall so vacantly she could have been a mannequin. She still wore the same hair band. "Anyways, see you next time, Greg."

Greg snorted, and they hopped out of the elevator into a large conference room paneled in fine, rich wood. There was a grand table surrounded by various diplomats from the Rimward Organizations, the Citlal and the Martians. At the head of the table, staring at a framed crowbar with her back to everyone, was the most dangerous woman in the universe: you, of course. Chess Mistress Hex, the mighty and feared. You didn't just run the largest criminal empire for everyone Rimward, you were also a legitimate business woman who owned at least one sub-corporation of Centro Systems, with many interests on Centro's home of Earth. Not many people knew that, and most who found out were dead. Kalingkata wasn't just anyone, though, and as he walked in you turned your head and gave the faintest smirk.

"Kalingkata, finally. We've been waiting for you."

"Your elevator is, like, really slow."

"Yes, I've been meaning to fix that." You swiped your hand over the table, and wood panels slid away silently to reveal hologram projectors which flickered to life and displayed a map of the solar system—including the blue dots symbolizing massive fleet encroaching on them, pushing into the red light of their own territory.

"As most of you are aware, the fleets of the extra-universal empire known to us as the Council, though the name is a bad choice honestly, have been advancing throughout the Rim. While our alliance has been effective in that we're all not completely dead, I'm sad to say we are losing. Our losses have far outstripped theirs, and unless we can come up with a new plan, the best we can hope for is a pyrrhic stalemate for a few years. Our defeat isn't immediate, it isn't dire, but we do need to face the fact that our current strategy is just plain not working."

There were a lot of downcast faces at this, and many more looking grim and fatalistic. None of them looked surprised. They'd all fought in wars before, some on Mars, some in deep space, and all sorts of places. They'd seen their foes play all sorts of tricks and games, and Kalingkata, Hotaru, Fei, Hex, Arch, Jade, Celeste, Natsu, Aequitas, Mikey, Shadow, Michael, Doitzel, Ellodie, and all their other friends had been able to push back the tide with cunning and tricks of their own. This time, though, the force attacking them had the subtlety of a bulldozer, and it was proving to be more effective than it had any right to be. *If only they would just try something clever, we'd be able to catch them off guard again for sure. That's what we always did,* Sang Ki thought to himself. But watching the hologram projection, he was forced to acknowledge that at this point, they couldn't count on that. "We need a new plan. Something to break the stalemate and push it into our favor. Which is why I've assembled you all here, of course."

Jenny looked at Sang Ki. He was gritting his teeth. "Something wrong?"

"Just a feeling."

There was a long silence, which was finally broken by the low sonorous voice of a Citlal.

"The adviser has a plan," Aequitas said.

"The adviser, as you call her, is certifiably insane,"

Sang Ki spat.

You smiled a little too politely. "She's immortal. She's had a lot of time to think about things."

Sang Ki turned to Jenny, "This is what I was worried about." He rose. "We really cannot trust Jade Darkshadow. The obvious first reason is she is a woman who chose to change her last name to Darkshadow, which is the most cartoonish sort of hint you can give your fellow beings that you might not have their best interests at heart. Not to mention she tried to get several people in this room killed, sometimes at her own hand, and is pretty much the absolute epitome of untrustworthiness. I'd know that better than anyone else."

You pursed your lips. "We're all very aware of the...relationship," Sang Ki clenched his hand tight at the word, "you two had. However, if she has a good suggestion, we should be open to it."

The plates of Aequitas' exoskeleton shifted as he turned his gaze on Kalingkata. "Ruthless action is exactly what is needed now. The Council must be broken. Are you any better than her, ordering war? Killing is part of the game, Kalingkata."

"I won't bother with the most basic 'don't become your enemy' argument, Aequitas. But you should know you cannot trust Jade."Kalingkata leaned in, "That you haven't let her being dead stop her from giving advice is both tragic and an abomination against nature."

You waved your hand. "Quiet, both of you. Did you bring her?"

Aequitas shifted his mass of plated body in what they'd grown to recognize as a nod, and another Citlal shifted into the room carrying a cube in its extended mouth pincers. The cube seemed to be as big as a person, its surface lined with tubes and veins. Inside, membranes shifted along with bone-like plates, bits of stone, and metal pistons.

"Jade. Always such a pleasure. How are you this afternoon??"

"Glad to be amongst the living!"

Natsu audibly shifted in his seat as the cube spoke.

"And you have something to say to us all today, I hear?"

Jenny leaned in. "Is that really her? They really did it?"

"They really did it." Kalingkata thought back to those days with the Citlal scientists, weaving the vat-grown flesh in with the machinery... "We," he corrected himself.

"That's her soul in there?"

"If she has one."

The cube spoke again. "Yes, Hexie, I have a lot to say actually, and I think you're very much going to like what it is." She began to speak, and kept speaking for a long time. By the time she had finished, there wasn't a being with jaws that didn't have them a little bit slack.

If Kalingkata hadn't been such a slight man, the way he slammed the door open as he walked out of the conference room would have looked extraordinarily threatening. As such, it didn't really, but at least he showed everyone he was displeased. Backgammon Jenny started to follow him before you, Chess Mistress Hex, grabbed her by the arm. "Jenny, could I have a word?"

"The boss is pissed, really pissed. No."

"I need to talk to you about Aladdin."

Jenny relaxed. "Okay fine, but only because it's about Aladdin."

You smiled. "I've learned a few things about the boy since he started interning for me. Secrets he doesn't want anyone to know. But more importantly, there are things

I've learned our enemies have learned as well. Things we might be able to play to our advantage in large ways."

"I don't like the way you're talking."

"What we've been doing here isn't working. Don't you want Aladdin to live a long and happy life? What if something happened to that new pal of his, whats her name, Songbird?"

"Nightingale."

"Right. I mean, this war has already cost him one friend. Would you really want another body weighing him down?"

FILE 3:
EVERYONE LOVES A LAD INSANE

Entry from Jhe Aladdin's personal diary. Copied exactly as written, including the quoted song lyrics (which I wouldn't be quoting if you weren't paying me, I hate that song.) By the way, stealing teenager's diaries is not the way I'd like to go about writing reports in the future, I mean I know we're a criminal empire and everything, but honestly it just feels kind of tacky and tasteless? Like, sure this is really relevant to the "plot" of this non-fictional narrative, but could I please do something else next time? This just feels like stealing candy from very influential children whom I am scared I am pissing off in the future.

* * * * *

You've gotta kid around
And run around with guns
But when the playtime's over
And you've run through all your fun
Gotta grow up sometime
And those new tales make you run
-Carnival Reichenbach, Childlike

My name is Jhe Aladdin. I'm a teenager, I'm ridiculously wealthy, my mom and dad saved the Universe, and my childhood friend is dead. Andromeda Phillips. Boom. After all those times playing war together as kids, war itself caught up to us in a very real way. My friend was alive and laughing, now somehow after all these years they just aren't there anymore, and here I am at Celeste's home ready to say my condolences.

I missed the funeral. I wish someone had told me.

* * * * *

"Bang!" said Andromeda. I fell to the ground, clutching my breast. "Take that, you filthy Corporate Centro Scum!"

My mom, dad, and Mr. and Mrs. Phillips were having tea, or something that looked like tea, they didn't look over.

"I guess I'm dead." I replied, staring up at the blue sky. "Where do we go from here?" I don't think Andromeda expected so much philosophizing. I was 5.

"Yes, you're dead," a voice said, "just like me. Now we have something in common, Aladdin."

"Shut up!" I yelled. Andromeda looked confused. I blushed. My parents looked over.

"Is everything okay over there?"

"Fine!" I yelled. "Sorry Andromeda." She helped me up. I remember the feel of her hand, the creases of it. Those creases are rotting now.

"Are you okay Aladdin?"

"Yeah. Sometimes I like to... pretend I talk to a ghost. It's like a game."

"Well that sounds fun. Let's be ghosts."

No, I thought, that's the last thing I want.

* * * * *

I sit with Celeste at the table. Her husband isn't home. Calling her Celeste is weird. She is still Andromeda's mom, Mrs. Phillips, not Celeste. That sounds so cold. So adult. It's like acknowledging her daughter isn't there. In a way, it's a relief none of the rest of the family is there. I couldn't look Andromeda's sister Ariadne in the face, and I wasn't even sure why. I hugged Celese when I came in the door. I brought flowers for the grave, and they sit on the table at an empty place setting for now. I can't help but wonder whose. I can't ask. I try to say something to make it better, but we just sit there in silence. I almost want the voice in my head to speak again. It stopped a few months back, after all those years.

* * * * *

My first memory of her was just her staring at me. I was too young to talk, and I accepted her as always there. She was a constant presence, following me around the home, and my world. Like an invisible friend. I thought everyone had one of her. Sometimes, though, she spoke.

"Hello Aladdin. Aren't you a strapping young man?"

"You can't be here, this is my dream."

"I'm always in your dreams."

She was taller than me, but not entirely a person. She was a shadow of a person. Residue. She was blonde. Her clothes were tailored. I could make out strange details even though she was a blur.

"I've been watching you since you were a little baby, talking to you after mommy put you to bed."

"I know. Get out of my head."

"I won't. And you don't have any control over that. How does that make you feel?"

"GET OUT OF MY HEAD!"

"Powerless? Is it cause you're just my puppet? My plaything? You're everything I ever wanted you to be. And you'll be more when you get older. You'll probably be quite handsome." She ran her finger along my back, but it wasn't really my back, it was the back of my mind. It quivered. I felt sick.

"Who are you?"

"I'm your Empress. Not of any body of land, but of life and death. And of you."

"I don't want you to be."

"That's not how this works."

We were in a city, baroque. We flew over it, I moved with her and we saw the same things from the same eyes. "This is a city I built in my mind, out of boredom. You do realize how pitifully little there is to do when you're dead? You don't sleep. You don't eat. There's nothing to break up the monotony unless you make it. And I made you."

The city was vast. People made of dreams slipped around beneath us. There was a man who was the memory of hand running along the fur of a cat, a woman made of a drop of blood hitting the ground, splashing up upon impact, and a child made of the dream of sitting in a throne. I passed over it all. We did. She held me too close.

"What am I then? Who am I?"

"You're playtime."

* * * * *

"Your mother and father must be so proud of you Aladdin, though I admit you take after Kalingkata way more than your mom. And you're a bit more of a Rimward than either of them." I try to ignore the end of that sentence.

"I hope they are too. Dad's training me to do his kind of work. I'm not sure how Mom feels about it."

"They'll be alright, your brother and sisters turned out alright." I take some solace in that. At least one kid can be the failure. I have that to fall back on. I turn to see if anyone is following us. No.

"Thanks Mrs. Phillips."

"Please, call me Celeste."

"Sorry, Celeste."

"It's okay, it's just, when you say that it makes me think of the two of you playing, and it makes me think that I was..." She starts crying. I hold her. I cry too. It takes a long time before we both stop, and it is cold by then, so I walk her back to the house and head for Andromeda's grave, flowers in hand. She didn't have to finish the sentence. I know it ended in, "her Mom."

* * * * *

Left, says the ghost. The other members of the crew of the Sefkrie are at my heels. I downloaded a map of the space station, but I'm only pretending to look at it. I'm following her. She knows how useful she is. I resent it.

We hit another fork. *RIGHT*, she yells. How does she know this place? She never mentioned it, and despite myself I feel I should know every detail of her. I hate myself for it. Nightingale is behind me with Ariadne. She trusts me to know where to go. I trust her to follow. Andromeda is there too, I've known her so long, but she hesitates when I parrot the orders.

Right. Left. Turn. Stop! Jump. Left. DUCK!

You can measure the time I've known Nightingale in hours.

She doesn't hesitate. She pulls Andromeda out of the way of the falling beam I said to duck from. She doesn't gloat, or even pause to recognise she just saved the girl's life. She just keeps running. Her body is lighting arcing across a lake.

There's something else, Aladdin... Something to

consider.

"Something wrong, Aladdin?" Nightingale asks.

I smile through the grime, "I'm fine, keep going."

She knows I'm lying instantly. She frowns just slightly. It's refreshing, purifying.

Nightingale was a welcome addition to my life. Though I'm embarrassed to say it. In some ways it feels like she arrived just in time for Andromeda to die. Sometimes I have dreams she is in, and I like them because the ghost never shows up in those dreams. She wouldn't appreciate me saying that. I don't think. Either way, I have serious mental health issues, at least according to Aunt Fei. I've been to a lot of therapy, but I'm not sure anything can change those dreams.

Nightingale listens. I trust her a lot, and I can't figure out why. She's older than me, grew up on Earth, and is the first mate on a pirate ship... Which doesn't even begin to touch on the topic of her friend David, a man I've never been sure was acting as her protective and assumed older brother, or unstated romantic rival. If you can even think of our relationship that way. Everyone around us calls it that. Do I? Either way, we leave a lot unsaid. The crew of the Sefkrie do their jobs, and I come aboard when I'm needed. I flitter in and out of their lives. David is a stable rock to the whole crew, and I know practically nothing about him.

There are few people who intimidate me. Ghosts do that to a person. David scares the bejesus out of me. I wish I could write how he looks at me. If I was a rolley-polley I'd curl up in a ball and hide when he does that. The thing is that he is ridiculously strong, kind, sacrifices himself for others, and has abs like a tank.

I can never measure up to him. I think that's what scares me.

When I was little my mother would sing me to sleep, and I'd look up and feel safe and loved. She would hold my tiny hand as she let me off for school, or my dad would. When I got older, they spent less time with me and more with business. I still had the Ghost to talk to.

Hanging out with Nightingale, Greed, Daivd, Ariadne and Andromeda, and their crew for that short time, I felt welcomed briefly into a family. I dreamed of going back there. I prayed I would go back there and see them all again.

Now Andromeda is dead.

* * * * *

She was at my windowsill. The drapes waved, as did her hair and her willowy clothes.

"How are you here?"

"I'm not, you're dreaming."

"I'm always dreaming."

She kissed me. I felt sick.

"I want you to understand something Aladdin."

"What's that?"

"Eternity. I want you to feel what it's like to die alone."

I was her. The Ghost. I walked in her shoes and my hair dangled down. I went into a room. I talked to a video

41

screen with another woman's face on it. I was catty. It was a blur then. There was gas. And I fell alone into an escape pod, and from the view screen watched the stars become endless, separated from the world. I was alone. My slender white hand touched the glass. I saw my skin and fingernails glow in the faint starlight.

And then the bombs went off. They ripped me apart, and I felt my body vaporize. In that moment, I saw my life flash before my eyes, sort of, her life, and scenes from a different life on Mars. They didn't make sense. There was a boy smiling. He was dead and a young man was standing over him. I was shooting him in the head in Chicago. My father pointed up at the stars, but I wasn't her anymore, I didn't know who I was. I saw a girl smile. We kissed. She died. I was in space, and I was vapor, and I was dead.

* * * * *

My father knocked on the door. I'm not sure how young I was. A woman opened the door, she had brown hair. She wrinkled her nose.

"Hi, I'm one of the most powerful people in the Universe. I brought my kid, can I come in and talk to your husband? I brought tea!" My father had spent the last twenty minutes thinking of the weirdest and yet most mundane thing he could say when we got to the door. We'd heated up the tea around the corner while people looked at us funny. I never questioned his methodology. We were let inside. He also brought cookies. A man, frankly fairly terrifying, came out. A man I recognized from stories, who I thought was a story like the tooth fairy. He was Greed. When the nice brown haired woman asked if I wanted to go play with Tobias, whoever that was, I followed her ushering unquestionably.

I told the other kids at school my dad brought Greed tea and cookies and cracked jokes with him. The other kids already knew my dad from the stories. They believed it.

Tobias was older than me, a little, and was playing with a group of metal spiders. It looked like they were dancing.

"What are those?"

"Who are you?"

"Aladdin. My dad's talking business or is giving away tea and cookies."

"Tobias, Tobias Greed. They're eye-ders."

I looked at one. Its singular namesake eye swiveled to look at me. It was shy, and backed away. Another one was more outgoing.

"Beat his face in." The Ghost said.

"They're all very distinctive. I name this one Earl."

"You can't do that, his name is Four."

"That's not a very creative name."

"Its his name though."

The eye-der stumbled around my palm, and up my arm. It tickled.

"Does your dad let you mess with them?"

Tobias grinned. "Let and do are different."

We were going to be great friends.

"Gouge his eye out. The left one." The Ghost said.

We played, though other children might have called it work.

"Time to go Aladdin, we've set the work up."

"Can we come back?"

"Aren't you scared?"

"I think it's a good idea to get on good terms with Greed, Daddy. Maybe you can get him to be generous."

We left, but Dad didn't stop laughing for some time.

* * * * *

"...Malcolm Carmichael!" She screamed. I woke up in a sweat. I could feel her smiling. I could hear her crying.

* * * * *

"You didn't do what I said. You should have hurt him."

"I didn't want to."

"You'll want to."

"You can't make me."

"You shouldn't have said that."

I found myself in a white room.

"Where am I?"

"You're in your head. And I'm going to leave you here Aladdin. I'm going to leave you here for a year."

"You can't leave me in here for a year!"
Silence.

"You can't, I'll need food. I'll die!"
Silence.

There was only silence. For a year. I can't really describe that. How alone I felt. How much I cried. How I screamed and yelled and carved notches into the walls every night.

It was 12 months later I heard another sound.

"Do you miss me?"

"Please let me out."

"I haven't locked you up anywhere. It's all here, inside your head. Aren't you the master of your own destiny Aladdin? Can't you make your dreams come true? Tell me you can't."

I was curled up on the cold floor, my tears puddling on the imaginary concrete.

"I can't. I can't."

"Good. Now tell me you're mine."

"I'm yours you can do whatever you want with me." I said, in between the gasps of tears.

"That's a good little boy. Who's your mommy, little boy?"

"My mommy?" It took me a moment "Hotaru Kowano is."

"No she's not. Not anymore. Tell me who your mommy is now, little boy."

I tried to wipe the tears away and make them stop. I knew what I had to say.

"You are. You are, Ghost lady. You're my mommy." I struggled to think of how to beg my way out of this and added, "Empress." I felt her laugh.

"My name is Jade Darkshadow little Aladdin. And I'm your mommy now. Welcome to the family."

I sat up. "So I can go?"

"I'll be back for you in a week."

"No!" The worst part was, while I waited those days out, I began to feel grateful she was letting me go. That she wasn't so bad. I hated myself for thinking that.

Seven days later, I woke up. It was the next morning. I ran to Hotaru and hugged her. "Hotaru Hotaru I'm so scared." She held me. And my heart slowed down. My real mommy. I could still hear the Ghost laughing. I didn't stop clinging for an hour. I told her it was a nightmare. After some time, I pictured the Ghost in my head, and my malice grew. "You're my mommy," I told my real mommy.

"Yes? I am," she replied. Good. I could feel the Ghost's anger ripple along my spine. I treasured that feeling.

* * * * *

My sister Kotone and I were skipping rocks at the stream. I wasn't very good, which means plainly, she was skipping rocks, and mine plopped in. I didn't want to learn. I got the impression the Ghost liked the violence of the kerplunk.

"You're doing it all wrong, Aladdin, you need to choose flat, smooth stones like this one."

"Yeah, sure." I picked up a big rock. It made a splash.

"Stupid brother."

I frowned.

"Sorry." She narrowed her eyes a bit. "How bout I show you?"

"Throw her into the river and push her face into the stream. Hold her there while she thrashes. Wait till she stops."

"Sure."

She showed me the rock, and how to hold it, and put her arm over mine and did the motion together till I got it down. It took me a few tries, but I got it down. We laughed together. I love my sister.

When we finished, she headed home first. I told her I'd be right behind her. I ran into the woods, the teal leaves of the Martian Olive trees batting my face. I ran and ran till my legs burned and my lungs were sore. I fell over.

"I'm not hurting anyone."

"You will. Or I'll put you back in the room."

"No. Please don't."

"I can do other things to you. Things you don't want to know."

"I'm sorry, I'm sorry Empress Darkshadow. I'm sorry."

"You should be. I want to see blood Aladdin. You're failing me. Get me some blood." I looked around, I was in the woods, there wasn't... There was a squirrel. I stared it down. I pulled out some bread I'd saved for the fish. My hand shook as I placed it on the ground. I felt my hand go around a rock.

"The room, Aladdin."

The squirrel skittered towards the bread and looked at it. It bit it. I smashed the rock down on it. Again. And again. And again. The tears ran down my face as the blood splattered me.

"Good boy Aladdin. Good boy."

* * * * *

Tobias, Andromeda and I looked down the hole.

"Who goes down first?" Tobias ventured.

"Not me," I muttered.

"Nose goes!" Andromeda spat.

Naturally, with my hands on my knees peering down the hole, I didn't do very well.

Tobias had the knotted rope ready, and my protestations that this wasn't safe were only met with the usual, "It's fine!" from my friends, and, "Hurt them horrifically," from the Ghost. The two of them held the rope, and I carefully climbed down, holding a flashlight in my teeth. If any of our parents found us, we were going to get so grounded. Though getting locked in my room full of things just didn't have the same bite anymore—not that I told my parents that.

The hole was fleshy, and I felt like I was climbing down someone's vein or nostril. We were on a Citlal ship. The climb took longer than I expected, but I reached the bottom, found my footing on the squishy ground, and untoothed my flashlight.

"Are you alive Aladdin?"

"Yeah!"

"What's down there?"

"Don't know yet!" I shined the light around. "There isn't much room down here—," The light shone on an alien and I stopped. Its eyes turned to face me, but not its torso. I'd met plenty of this kind of alien before. It was a Citlal, aliens who'd popped in from another reality and decided to ally with the Martians and Rimwards. It seemed shorter than usual, and I quickly learned why: it was being held down by thick bonds. Its long body stretched back along what looked like a simple metal board with wheels. Is long slithering body had been nailed to the board. The Citlal used its nose to push the cart around the room, and turned itself towards me.

"WHAT ARE YOU DOING DOWN HERE, CHILD?"

"...exploring...."

"SPEAK UP BOY."

"Exploring!"

It nodded. Its voice softened, "A noble venture. I hear you have companions, are they joining us?"

I was going to say no, but I heard their grunts climbing the rope. I just hoped they didn't secure the rope by tacking to the living floor.

"AH, I SEE THEY HAVE JOINED US."

Tobias and Andromeda shined their flashlights on the Citlal.

"Look at it! I've never seen anything like it!"

"Don't be silly Andi, you've seen lots of Citlal."

"Not on wheels!"

"IT'S MY FITTING PUNISHMENT FOR BETRAYING MY PEOPLE. I HOPE YOU NEVER SUFFER SUCH A FATE AS HAVING YOUR LIMBS TORN OFF AND BEING FORCED TO LIVE IN A DARK HOLE."

I could agree with all of that.

"What do you do here?"

"WHAT I AM GOOD AT, COME, TAKE A LOOK." He ushered us with his paw, and we slowly stepped forward. Hidden by the Citlal's massive form and the shadow was a canvas of fleshy matter and vines. The Citlal delicately pulled a tubelike growth and slid it into a stitch he had cut in another plant.

"What is that?" Tobias couldn't take his eyes off, none of us could.

"Plant weaving. If you know the way to, you can create living works of art from plants. It's a long and storied art form of the Citlal — one few know how to do — and the only reason I deserve to live." His voice had softened. "I am creating a portrait of our Chief, Aequitas. One that will live forever, even if he doesn't, as long as it is properly watered and fed."

"It doesn't look anything like Aequitas," Andromeda murmured.

"It won't for a few more months. The plants must grow together and be tended precisely. It is not an art for the impatient."

The logistics of it flooded my brain. "Do you even control the plants' reproductive cycles to ensure it remains the same?" If a Citlal could smile, he did.

"You are clever, child. Creating a plant weave is creating an ecosystem. You must learn to become like the Ancestors, patient and tender, but merciless when you need to be."

I am not a touchy feely person, and I wasn't sure about my companions, but we just stood there, holding hands, watching the master carefully move and assemble the picture. We watched together for hours. It was the most beautiful thing I'd ever seen.

Hours later when the shipwide alert found us in a hole watching art, it was also the most trouble I'd ever been in. As the Citlal security carted us off, I did get to ask one more question.

"What's your name?"

"I have renounced all names since my failure. But I may be given one."

"Call him Earl." Tobias smirked.

"Earl indeed." I replied.

"Why Earl?" Andromeda said, confused.

Tobias and I shared a glance before we were rushed back into the arms of angry parents.

We visited again, and often.

* * * *

Nightingale groaned as Andromeda and I dropped her on her bed.

"I could have made it by myself, you didn't need to waste the effort."

Andromeda rolled her eyes, "Nightingale, you literally jumped in front of a club."

"Lots of people do that. You wouldn't worry about cricket teams."

Andromeda looked at me, frowning, "I'll go get the medi-gel."

The ghost giggled, "Finally, we're all alone. She has secrets. You know she hasn't told you everything."

Shut up. Shut up shut up shut up.

"Why how rude Aladdin!" Jade replied.

Nightingale tried to sit up, "My father wouldn't let this stop him."

I reached out and touched her hair, just as I suspected not all of the red was her natural hair color. "Nightingale, I think you were hit more than once."

"I'm fine, really." She tried to rise again.

Gently, I touched her hand, "Tell me about your father."

She really was looking delirious at this point, and I knew I needed to keep her from getting up.

"He was... Is... Kind. I left him behind, Aladdin. On Earth. They were counting on me there, the resistance against Centro... And I abandoned them. My father is rotting in prison and I can't do anything about it. I..."

"You didn't abandon them. You did what you had to do. You're alive, and as long as you're alive, you can do so

52

many things."

Oh, aren't you so right, Aladdin.

Quiet.

Ha.

"Aladdin, even if it wasn't your fault...if you weren't there to help someone you love when they're in danger... it feels like it is. I'll blame myself forever if he dies."

"I've got the medicine," Andromeda said, running into the room.

"Don't you worry, Nightingale, no one is dying on our watch."

* * * * *

I kneel down in front of Andromeda's grave. I set the flowers there, and say prayers for her. I pray for her soul, for her parents, for me, for my family, for my friends. And I pray that God please listen because we need it. The wind blows over the grave, and her tombstone stares blankly back at me. And I am alone. There is no ghost. There is no Andromeda. No anyone. Just me and this gravestone. I think of Nightingale and how she gave a shit about me, and then I think about how awful her life was. I thought about David, and what pain he has to be going through every day with those body modifications, and I wonder if I was just as much an intruder into Tobias' ship as the Ghost was in my life.

"Just come out already!" I scream. "Just talk to me! Where are you, you stupid goddamn Empress of nothing? Come out already! Talk to me! TALK TO ME! PLEASE!" I scream and cry into the ground. Andromeda is dead. She'll

never go and visit Earl with me again. She'll always be
dead. The Ghost is gone. And I am alone.

I pull my face up from the dirt and wipe my tears off. I
can't be this weak. Not if I don't want to go back to the
room. I stand up. And dust myself off.

"Goodbye Andromeda." I kiss the tombstone. "You
used to shoot me down."

Research Sketch:
Jhe Aladdin

-Youngest son of Jhe Sang Ki and Vacuum heiress Hotaru Kowano.

-Has four siblings.

-Intern to you.

-Makes great coffee.

-Childhood trauma related to the "deceased" Jade Darkshadow.

-A bit pretentious, but hey he's a teenager.

Carl Fredrickson

FILE 4:
ESPIONAGE

There were two people in the elevator shaft on the abandoned station, one leaning into it, carefully lowering the rope down the shaft that was tied securely to a water fountain on the wall. She wanted to wipe her brow, but if she took one hand off she'd let too much of the rope down.

"You really could let me do that Half-Pint," said the man standing behind her. She flashed a grin at him, and then brought her focus back to the elevator shaft. "No can do David This is my responsibility, not to mention you're supposed to be taking care of the Council expedition team."

David crossed his arms and leaned on the metal wall. "Already done. Caught two of them while they were sleeping, killed the other one pretty quietly, too."

She sighed, "Not a particularly honorable way to kill them off." She yelled the new information down the shaft.

"Half-Pint, what matters is we survived and they're dead." She halfheartedly nodded—it wasn't really the time to debate this. She kept lowering the rope, until all of a sudden her eyes went wide and the rope slipped and jerked down. She tightened her grip and felt the rope burn her palms a bit.

"That kind of hurt!" a voice yelled up from far lower in the shaft.

"Sorry Aladdin!"

"What's got you spooked Half-Pint?"

"David, I could swear Aladdin said he'd counted four guards when he hacked the cameras."

He shook his head. "Definitely three. I remember specifically."

Nightingale tried to reassure herself. "Yeah, you're probably right..."

Jhe Aladdin jerked on the rope and felt the nausea from the sudden whiplash flow over him. "Ow!" He yelled up involuntarily. The rope started lowering again normally. Nightingale was doing a pretty good job, one slip-up wasn't anything awful. His feet hit the concrete at the bottom of the hole, and he undid the harness on his torso and tugged twice on the rope to let Nightingale know he'd hit the bottom safely. Now to do his job. The station had once been part of the the monitoring stations set up during the great alternate reality portal experiments, then it was abandoned during the following conflict. The Council had sent some sort of delegation to the empty station, and it was Aladdin's job to find out why. Easy enough job. All he had to do was get to a terminal linked to the main computer and dump the data. Of course, because of how ridiculously competent the best hackers were, the station had been built with its main computer able to cut itself off from subsidiary computers any time it detected malicious action on its systems. This meant he had to go spelunking to find an unguarded terminal, or go in guns blazing. They didn't know how many soldiers of the Council were in the place to begin with, so decided it was best to go with caution. They knew the number was at least four, and they'd taken out three...

Aladdin walked down the hallway, the air stale, and heard a gentle growling from his left. The creature was one he'd seen before, its hide scales of rusting iron, its eyes yellow with four pupils. Its three jaws opened and it gave a staggering, pulsating cry. Then it leapt at him. Aladdin cried out himself and bolted down the hallway, his shoes splashing in pools of oil and hydraulic fluid. If I was him I probably would have cowered in fear, but let's be real—that was not the best course of action here. He was terrified, though watching the footage of him running through the hallway after the fact, knowing he gets out alive, is comical. The creature's terrifying metal paws that could rip his skin to shreds splash through the oil puddles like it's playing in them. Aladdin's lanky arms and legs pump with Olympic level dedication. Put Benny Hill music over it. It's fantastic.

The creature corners him. His hands go to the wall. He looks up. The creature stalks towards him, thick dark fluid dripping from its jaws.

From above it: bullets. Nightingale drops down, one hand holding onto the rope as she slides down it, the other emptying shells into the creature. She drops onto its back, jamming the gun between the plates of the creature's hide and fires. It drops to the ground dead.

It's a quick and brutal ending to the scene.

"You okay Aladdin?" she asked.

"Yeah, just a little spooked." He put his hands on his knees and took a deep breath. "Alright, wanna chaperone me to the target?"

She bowed and held an arm out towards the destination, "It would be my honor." They walked through the cold hallway, "How long do you think you'll be on the ship this time?" Nightingale asked.

He shrugged, "Not sure, honestly. Could be weeks, could be days."

"What happens when you leave, I mean..." she pursed her lips, "when you leave it never quite feels real. I think of you as part of our crew, but..."

"But really I'm just the hired help. Filling in a role you're missing when you need it."

"That's not true, we love having you on board. Well, at least I do."

"I think that's just cause, you know?"

"Do I?"

He looked away, "A lot of the crew had normal lives. We... didn't. We suffered. You had to leave your family and go into exile, pretend to be a mercenary instead of a political revolutionary. You spent your whole life in protests and fights... What I'm trying to say is neither of us really had a childhood. I mean, we did but... It was a different one than most people have."

She looked straight ahead, "Yeah, I suppose you're right. Even better we keep track of each other then. With Andromeda gone..."

"Yeah."

"Yeah... So, I hope you stick around."

"I hope so to."

"But if you don't, will you be okay on your own?"

He waved her off, "Psh, I'm always okay."

They reached the terminal, where Aladdin extracted all of the data from the base's systems, including the security footage I watched. They then exited the facility, and climbed out to the surface, walking back to the Sefkrie. They weren't alone.

A shuttle marked with the symbols of the Index was parked nearby, and your aide Alexis stood outside it. She waved to Aladdin.

He frowned at Nightingale, "Well, till next time then, Alice MacLeod."

"Till the next time, Jhe Aladdin."

Carl Fredrickson

Research Sketch:
Alice "Nightingale" MacLeod

-First mate on the spaceship, "The Beard of Zeus."
-Exile from Centro territories, including her home of Earth.
-(Former?) Member of the "Working Class Heroes" insurgent group on Earth.
-Not a cat person.
-Daughter of an activist and a Centro soldier.
-Has a helluva reward on her head.

FILE 5:
THE SON OF THE KING OF WEBS

Alexis had shut the door on his room on the shuttle, the same one that ferried him to every job he worked for the Index. This time it was some conference or something, he lost track. It was night, as much as it could be night in space where night and day were only concepts in your head. It was time to sleep, and so it was night. And on this, like every night, he stared up at the moving star patterned tiles above his bed, and wondered why people were born under starlight, and what his life would have been like if all the stars he looked at above him weren't tiles. He closed his eyes.

"Shh," Nightingale said, and she popped the tab on the grape soda and put it to his lips.

"Why is it grape?"

"Why are you asking?"

"Because this is a lucid dream. And you're not here."

"And you're spending too much time with Hexie."

"And you're not here."

"And you know I'm right."

"And I wish you were here."

"But isn't this what I'd say?"

"That's good grape soda." He sipped it through his dreams. "And you're right."

And that was always how it was with the girl of his dreams in his dream.

And then there is me, who isn't a girl. I'm Carl Fredrickson, one of the Senior Espionage Analysts who work with Kalingkata and you. I'm not a spy, of course. That would just be silly.

"So I'm a spy?" I asked Kalingkata during my job interview.

"Don't be ridiculous. Hexie and I both tried spying on each other, but we figured out who the other's spies were and then all the espionage just turned into a game of feeding false info that spelled out dirty limericks if you took the first letters of every word and that sort of thing. It got out of hand. Hexie and I don't spy on each other. We have Senior Espionage Analysts who try and sneak all the info out from the other's organization they can, and everyone knows who they are, and no one tries to kill them in their sleep. You'll even get invited to Hexie's corporate picnics, and let me tell you, they're damn good picnics."

"Why on earth would you let each other have paid spies in your bases you know about?"

"It's better than having paid spies you don't know about! We're all friends here. I went to one of Hexie's Senior Espionage Analysts' son's Bar Mitzvahs last month.

So don't think you're James Bond."

"Who?"

"Look, just spy on her politely. She might even ask you to tea."

And that's how I became a not really spy.

It's also how I became the narrator of this story, and first met Kalingkata's son Aladdin. Most of my employment was stealing your schematics or donuts, usually both from the break room, and chilling around the water cooler. Every so often you would call me over to your home for tea, which I would never be the only guest for (I wasn't that important) and it was there that I first met Jhe Aladdin. He was a young man, about 17, wearing glasses that kept having little blips of light appear on them as we talked, clearly giving them away as transparent computer screens. He wore a finely tailored suit that apparently had been bought for him by you, since I couldn't imagine the kid buying it himself. He struck me as the kind of kid who'd rather be performing covers of old Earth rock songs on a dirty stage and then eating filet mignon for dinner. That is, a bright young man with too much money who enjoyed slumming.

The other guests that day were a stunning blonde girl wearing an outfit reminiscent of something between a 1920s flapper, a pharaohess, and a grungy mechanic (if that makes any sense), an older man with a waxed mustache, a war hardened Caucasian man in a trench coat, an Indian girl who looked like she'd walked straight out of a cyberpunk fashion shoot and stared wide-eyed at everything around her, and finally a young black man who wore worn down by reality jeans, a T-shirt that said "24601" and a blue costume jacket like an 1800s soldier. They were quite the motley crew, sitting on the floor

Nipponese style (which the cyberpunk girl didn't entirely understand) and drinking what smelled like Earl Grey from English tea cups.

"Ah, Carl, welcome. You're just in time. I figured I'd let you sit in on this meeting, even though your boss' son is already here."

I met Aladdin's gaze, and it was an odd sensation because from the dots that popped up on the screen-lens glasses over his eyes, I could tell he immediately started a search on me. "Carl Fredrickson? Good to meet you." He extended a hand. "Jhe Aladdin."

"A pleasure."

"But let me make the rest of the introductions. Welcome to the annual Rimward Accord trade summit," you cut in.

"I apologize for Bowie de Anhault Dessau not being able to make it in person," said 24601 boy. "He's caught up on Earth."

"Understandable of course," you purred. "This is Jehovah Rhineheart of the Bourgeois-ZZ-Tops. This," she gestured to flapper pharaoh Grease girl, "is Cleopatra Hypercube of the Cube2HyperGang shipping company, here representing the Olympian Government."

"My dad says hi and shit," she mentioned.

"I bet he does," you smiled. "Maximum Robespierre, who needs no introduction." The man bowed his head in recognition, an irresistible twinkle in his eye. "Screw Top Sarah from the Valkyries," Sarah smiled at everyone like she was surprised someone knew her name. "Kevin Dirgge from the JJE," he barely moved in recognition, "and of course Jhe Aladdin and Carl Fredrickson of the Spinneret, and myself." You didn't need to say your own name, especially amongst such a team of b-listers. I was impressed Robespierre came in person, and that two of the Rim Orgs had sent their own children, but it was really impressive that as many of the Rim Orgs had managed to send a representative at all. Not all of them had, but I doubted all of them still entirely existed, let alone had the extra manpower to attend a cushy tea meeting. The war was harsh on everyone.

The meeting itself was pretty blasé, with everybody around the short table requesting some sort of deal from another person at the table. There was quite a lot of bickering, but it was notable how coolly Aladdin handled himself amidst the chaos. There was a glint in his eye like he was another person. He steamrolled over others' arguments, renegotiated contracts, but always made sure he wasn't screwing anyone or his own side over. This was a war after all. I mainly took notes. However, things got interesting when Trevon Yorr came in.

"I'm sorry I'm late," he said, his broad shoulders weren't built like an ox—the ox probably would ask if he wanted to use the plow to make the work go faster. His muscles were like woven pythons, and his red hair was in a buzz cut. The uniform he wore was almost Corporate Earth, but could clearly be spotted as—

"Trevon Yorr, Earth Resistance Forces. I'm here representing Admiral Cornelia Carthage."

Much of the room stared in shock, including Aladdin, whose eyes practically disappeared behind the number of tabs he pulled up on his glasses. The only exception was Jehovah, who stood up and embraced Trevon Yorr. Earth people are so touchy feely.

"So Trevon Yorr, how goes the glorious revolution?"

"Not very glorious, the Council has changed everything. I'm hesitant to be here, but war makes strange bedfellows."

"Do you know MacLeod?" Aladdin cut in a bit too quickly. You barely began to raise an eyebrow—no one else noticed, but occasionally one of your muscles goes rogue and I can get a read off you. Occasionally. Unfortunately it's usually impossible to tell from a muscle spasm.

"I do indeed know MacLeod, and his daughter."

The negotiations after that were...interesting. Aladdin worked diligently to sway shipping contracts in Trevon Yorr's favor. He was slick, that's for sure. I was pretty sure that a few of the people walked away from the table feeling good about themselves and woke up the next morning wondering what the hell they had agreed to, but it wasn't extortion. Just a narrower profit margin than any sane negotiator takes. Except our own contract—Aladdin just went to town on that. I'm not sure if we broke even with it or flat out lost money, but that was the first moment I realized the MacLeod name meant something important to Aladdin—and also where I leave this story, just as I enter it. Well, mostly.

I'm not a rich man, but I am better at my job than you think I am, Hex. Thanks to bugs, interviews, stolen data cards, bribery, hacked video footage, and all sorts of fun stuff, including alcohol induced confessions, I've pieced this story together. All the dialogue as it appears is word for word as it was said, and all paraphrased pieces of dialogue are from a secondary source, and hence less reliable. Hopefully we all live through this war, and I'll be able to sell this for massive amounts of dough when it's over. Fingers crossed.

Research Sketch:
Carl Fredrickson (Me!)

-Born on Oberon, the moon of Uranus. Went to college on its sister moon of Titania.

-Parents are Dan Fredrickson and Raavi Sridhar

-The best person for this job.

-Tired of getting blackmailed into doing jobs like this.

-Please pay me more.

-Great facial hair.

Carl Fredrickson

FILE 6:
A GAME OF MURDERS

Now, I spent a lot of time going through who was at that tea party, and there was a good reason for it. Some of them don't live through this chapter. Also, the tea party wasn't the only function they were attending. You rarely do public events, but after the meeting you were throwing some sort of war time gala. It wasn't entirely clear what the focus of it was to me. You were sort of selling War Bonds, sort of bringing Martian, Rimward, and Centro diplomats together, sort of holding a giant information coup, and sort of just throwing a party. I am quite certain that whatever your real intentions were, you wanted to make sure no one else was certain of them.

"Now Aladdin," you said behind your dressing screen as you tried on dresses, "this is going to be your time to shine. There will be a lot of important people at this meeting, and I want you to get everything you can out of them."

"I'd figured that before you said it, Hexie."

"Good boy, Aladdin. You're like a wish come true."

"No magic lamp jokes."

"I wasn't going to make any," you smirked.

"I doubt that."

"Oh don't let it rub you the wrong way. I'm teaming you up with one of my agents. She's one of the best... and!" She poked her head around the screen. "She's cute. What with your whole hormone thing I figured you'd like that."

"I don't think you quite—"

"Look, this is a very important night, and I'm trusting you. You've done your job splendidly so far." Aladdin nodded, and looked down at the tablet computer he was jotting down notes on. There was a tab there with a bird on it. It said no new messages. He glanced at it repeatedly.

"I'll do my best, Hexie."

You called me to your house. It was the middle of the night, and if that wasn't odd enough, you had called me to talk to her alone. All of these were new things. When I got there, I was put through several security scans, and let through the garden door by a blank-eyed servant, who led me to a drawing room where you stood facing a window, your hands behind your back, the wind blowing a tree ominously. You had framed yourself like a painting when I entered, and I got chills. You were good.

"Sit down, Carl," you gestured at a specific chair. Neither statement nor action was a request. I took a seat. "You've hacked into all of my private bugs, and private video feeds."

I was scared, more scared than I'd ever been in my life. "That's my job, Mistress Hex."

"Do you know why you have been allowed to do this?" My brain swirled with things to say, but all that came out was me parroting back a word at her.

"Because you and Kalingkata have an agreement about espionage?"

"That's only the tip of this. You couldn't have hacked those firewalls unless I wanted you to. And now that you are in, I want you to do a job for me. One that will stay between us."

"I'd rather die than betray Kalingkata."

"Yes, he has that effect of people. Sometimes I think Jade died because she knew she would betray him if only she lived long enough, and she wanted to get it over with. But then I remember she wasn't deep enough for that level of emotional turmoil. No, you won't be betraying him. Quite the opposite. You'll be doing him a favor."

"What kind of favor?"

"Do you think being the Librarian is my only aspiration, Carl?" You walked towards a cabinet and took out a bottle of fine brandy. Or something like brandy. It was dark. You poured yourself a glass, but did not drink it. You had yet to show me your face.

"No, I don't think you'd limit yourself to that."

"Clever boy. Now, who do you think would take over here if I left?" You sipped, I shrugged.

"Lucian?"

She laughed. "Not nearly devious enough, darling. I need someone more talented." It was, of course, obvious. "You want me to spy on Jhe Aladdin."

"Not just spy. Compile. I don't have the time to watch hours and hours of footage of him. I'm a busy woman. You'll be handing me the Cliff Notes version of an assignment I'll be sending him on, an assignment I have very, very carefully bugged, wired, tapped, and made accessible in every way possible. Aladdin is bugged. He knows, of course, that if I want to I can hear what he hears and see what he sees. He also knows I don't really care. But I will next week. So that's your assignment—Cliff Notes. And make sure the story is a good one. I'll be sending you money for bribes to get any background info you need, and you'll also have access to some of my archives, so feel free to clear up any old cases you were wondering about for Kalingkata while you're there."

"Understood...I'll get right on it, Mistress Hex." I got up and headed for the door.

"Oh, and Carl?" I turned, and your hair swung as you turned your head, your eyes filled with a look of utter blood-drenched seriousness—the kind of vicious bloodthirstiness you'd imagine a killer having. "Carl, if you tell anyone about this little job, I will kill you, and I will get Kalingkata to want to kill you, too. I will kill your family, or enslave them, and I will make sure none of your deaths are fast or easy. Are we clear?" You smiled like a loving mother.

"Yes, Mistress Hex. Very clear."

* * * * *

Aladdin was meeting Aegenor for the first time then, in an abandoned ship dock that only had air because the atmosphere generators were solar powered and there were hobos around smart enough to fix them up. Aladdin had been dropped off by cab, as he'd been told his new partner would be driving to meet him. She was half an hour late, and Aladdin was tempted to start walking home when he heard the hum of an engine and the car roared in from the distance. It was an old one but not a classic, a dented up 2360s model with quite a few junkyard parts that had never been painted to match up. The car skidded to a halt, and a black haired white girl with a line of pierced rings down her cheek, a tight fitting turtleneck, a bulky cargo vest, and cargo pants got out. "You Jhe Aladdin?"

"I am. You Aegenor Valor?"

"Yeah," she muttered, wiping her nose on the back of her hand as she stepped toward him. Aladdin extended a hand. She punched him in the face. He staggered back, blood streaming from his nose.

What the hell?!"

"Welcome to the Index, bitch boy." She punched him in the stomach, and he bent over in pain.

"Thought you'd be a little pus. The Librarian always teams me up with your kind. Skinny little hacker boys—"

Aladdin ran forward and head-butted her into the car. It sounded like a rib broke.

"You little shit!" She kneed him in the chin, and the click of his teeth timed perfectly with the sudden impact as he fell to the ground, which didn't last long. She tried to kick him and he grabbed her leg, not only pulling her down, but also sinking his teeth into her.

"Let go of my leg!" She tried to beat him off, but he just bit down harder, like a wolf. She could see the blood staining her khaki cargos. "Fine, I'm done fighting. Just get the hell off me!" He let go, stood up, and spat her blood and his own out of his mouth. His face was a mess.

"Let's try that again." He extended a hand. "Jhe Aladdin."

"Aegenor Valor." She shook his hand. She spat in his face.

He wiped it off. "That's very nice. I see you're very eloquent."

She spat again.

"What the hell is wrong with you?" he yelled, and then spat a bloody gob of spit at her. She hadn't thought that through well enough.

"I guess we're working together," she said as she wiped the bloody spittle from her eye.

"I guess we are. I see we're off to a great start."

"I just wanted to get you used to life in Rimward space. I know very well who you are—a rich piece of trash trying to get in on our world. Never even killed someone before."

Aladdin looked at her very seriously from behind his cracked spectacles. "I served on a pirate ship for my last job for the Librarian. You'd be surprised what we had to do, there's a war on against the Council in case you forgot. Also, while you were punching me, I took your grenades from your pockets." He dumped them on the ground at her feet. "So, how do you say it in Rimward space? Hmn, I'm unfamiliar with the lingo, but I think the term is, 'Shut the hell up Aegenor?' Yes, that's it." He walked over to the passenger side of the car. "We leaving or not?" She glared at him and got in.

Aegenor is the same age as Aladdin, only about a month older or younger depending on which birthday I found listen for her is right. She was born on the streets of Mimas, and didn't exactly get along well there. Her mom and dad were both alive, which meant she couldn't go to one of the Darkshadow memorial orphanages. Sometimes she wished her mom and dad would just abandon her so she could go and get an education. She tried running away a few times, but that only led to heavier beatings, and she soon found it was easier to spend her time wandering the streets stealing and fencing things to the small time gangs then it was to learn about math or science. She beat up her first boy at the age of 7, and she beat up anyone she could after that. She lost her virginity at the age of 12 to a

16 year old, because she thought it would make her cool. When it didn't, she beat the shit out of the girls who called her a slut until they either shut up, or didn't have any teeth left for her to knock out. At fourteen she met an Index recruiter, and impressed him by beating up his body guard. She was hired on the spot. Since then she hasn't seen her parents or her siblings, and she drives her car around the moon beating the shit out of anyone her boss wants. She's great with her fists, great with a gun, great with a sword, great with being silent, great with stealing. Less great on talking or socializing. Still not satisfied with where she is.

Aegenor and Aladdin went to a combination clinic/greasy spoon called "The Nommy Cleric." You could get a fish stick and chips basket with a cola and a checkup for only twelve creds. The franchise was definitely going places. The public place had the added bonus of ensuring they would begin a professional conversation.

"So," Aladdin said, holding an ice pack to his face, "what exactly is our mission?"

"We're going to a gala the Librarian set up. You'll be my date. We're to gather intel from a list of targets, and if anyone starts trouble, take care of it."

Aladdin nodded. "Great, do you know how to dance?"

"I can dance better than you, I bet."

"Ballroom dance."

She was silent for a moment. "...Yes?"

"Okay then, show me. Let's waltz." Aladdin stood up, and held out his hand, Aegenor looked at it, took it, and got up. Aladdin slipped his hand around her waist, and she slapped it away.

"It's part of the dance."

"I know. Just didn't want you to get any ideas." They

were closer together than she'd like, but she had to improvise fast and learn the dumb dance, despite the awkward looks of the waiters, other patrons attached to IVs, and the guy at the register. Aladdin moved his feet, and she stumbled around. He had to be enjoying this, she thought, but he held his face calm and collected.

"One, two, three," he whispered, and suddenly the whole thing was very obvious. She wasn't into the whole following thing, but it was part of the dance and she was getting paid, so she adapted pretty quickly and soon enough, the two of them were twirling down the aisle. Aladdin was surprised how much tightly wound muscle he felt on her, like she was an Olympic athlete. Aegenor was not at all surprised by how little muscle she felt on him. "Well then, I think we'll be in good shape if you also know the foxtrot, and the—"

"Okay fine. I don't know any of these, but can we practice them not in the diner? I'm going to knock over someone's IV."

"Artesanal antibiotics on the house? The manager loved the entertainment," a waiter said, holding out a tray of pills.

They took the pills. "Here's to no infections," Aladdin said with a smirk.

"Cheers, or whatever," she replied.

Maybe this partnership wouldn't go so badly after all.

* * * * *

"I hate this, I hate you, I hate this dress, and I hate champagne." She downed the rest of the glass and set it back on the server's tray. "I apologize to the champagne, actually."

"Ha. Ha." Aladdin followed her through the crowd. "You need to remain more calm when people hit on you."

"I didn't hit him."

"That is a blessing, but you did throw champagne in his face."

"A waste. I could be tipsy by now, but I'm only buzzing."

"That's wonderful, and I'm sure your backwater charm will win over the hearts and minds of..." he maneuvered around a waiter, "all of the diplomats, but we really need to go back and talk to more of them."

She turned around. "The Librarian is playing some mean game pairing me with you?"

Aladdin pushed his glasses back to the ridge of his nose, which was still bruised, but thanks to high-end makeup didn't look so at all. "Indeed they are. It's a pretty obvious test. I searched you, you know. I know all about your record with the Index. I think the Librarian wants to see what both of us are made of."

She looked at him like a man about to kick a dog. "You're right. Let's go talk to the diplomats."

Aladdin held his elbow out to her, and she roped her arm around it more daintily than he expected. Dinner would be soon, but guests were supposed to assemble their plates at the buffet and take them to the tables to start eating only after the host took the first bite.

They wandered until Aladdin saw someone he recognized. "Cleopatra Hypercube?" The beads braided in Cleopatra's hair rattled as she turned. She was holding a roll in her teeth, and in her hand was a plate full of rolls with her name and the number of rolls on it scrolling in green letters.

"MMM HMN?" She said. Perfect ease-in, thought Aladdin.

"Cleopatra Hypercube, meet Aegenor Valor."

"Pleasure. Finally," Aegenor said, shaking her hand.

"MMESSURE" Cleo said around the roll. She bit off some, and grabbed the rest with her free hand. "I met you at the conference? You're Kalingkata's kid, yeah?"

"That I am. Aegenor, this is the daughter of Geraldine and Michelangelo Hypercube."

"Is that your real last name?"

Cleo shrugged. "I dunno. You know, Aladdin, you remind me of two of my siblings."

"Indeed?"

"Ulysses and Anya. You kinda look like Ulysses, ya know, cause he's half Martian from before my folks met, but I feel like you've also got some Anya in your eyes. It's funny."

I've never met them, so I can't tell you. I've always wanted to meet your parents, but my Dad would never let me."

"That's weird. Our mom never let us meet him either."

Aegenor looked back and forth between the two of them, as Cleo and Aladdin shared a weird look.

"What a weird coincidence. My dad probably pissed your parents off back in the day."

"Or vice versa..." The two of them laughed.

"So what brings you to this conference?" Aegenor was very tired of their chatter.

"Well, it's hard to do business without the Index. The Librarian has most of it locked up and..." Cleo put her hand on her stomach. "I don't feel so good."

"Well you were carrying that roll around in your teeth forever, girl, that can't be—"

"...Really not good."

Aladdin grabbed the roll from her hand and smelled it, then handed it to Aegenor, who smelled it as well.

"It's fucking poisoned," Aegenor exclaimed.

"My thoughts exactly, Cleopatra you need to throw up."

"I don't know how to do that!"

"Let me." Aegenor, in one swift motion put her fingers in Cleopatra's mouth, and her other hand rammed her stomach. There was a gagging sound, and then Cleo puked over Aegenor's hand, onto the fancy carpet. The guests nearby looked over.

"Aw geez Cleo, you had way too much champagne, let's go sit down," Aegenor said. Aladdin and Aegenor led her to some chairs in the corner, and Aladdin grabbed some water, which he tested with one of the poison/acid test strips that he kept around to test your coffee every morning.

"Wash your mouth out. You already puked, so just spit on the floor. Hopefully everyone thinks you're drunk,"Aladdin said.

Thanks," she muttered, then swished and spat. Aegenor wiped her hand off on the carpet until a server came around with a complimentary towel.

"I need to make a call." Aladdin touched Aegenor's shoulder as he got up, and she knew who he was calling.

"Hex?"

"Yes, my dear?"

"We have a serious problem."

"A Hypercube threw up on your date? I saw that."

"Poison."

"That's a bit more serious."

"I checked the rolls, they aren't all poisoned. So it's targeted. Probably something that can be added via liquid and evaporates quickly. We need to get people out of here."

There was a hacking sound and a thud, then a scream, and another.

"I think it's too late for that."

Screw Top Sarah, young as she was, was lying on the floor, foam dribbling from her mouth. A piece of cake was still in her hand, the finest she had ever gotten to taste before. Food was dropped by other guests as they stared in horror, and security rushed in.

"Well this isn't going according to our plan," Aladdin understated.

"Or theirs. I think they intended a timed launch. No one was supposed to be eating their food yet, just taking it to their tables from the buffet."

"The two who got it were the ones who didn't know or care."

"Exactly. Always invite mooks to your banquets for this exact reason, Aladdin."

He cringed a bit. "So, what exactly are we going to do?"

"The same thing we do every night, Aladdin. Not die."

"I mean about the murder."

"I'll get the guests in order. You are going to go and find out how everyone was poisoned."

"Aye aye, Hexie. Send someone over here to get Cleopatra medical attention." He hung up, and Aegenor looked over at him. She was rubbing Cleopatra's back.

"So, what's the news?"

"We're becoming detectives, apparently. But we won't have to be very good ones."

"Why's that?"

"Because I already know how they were planning on

killing their targets, we just need to know who they are now."

"And how were they planning it, since you're so smart?"

Aladdin walked over to the buffet table, and stuck his hand over it. The thing scanned his hand, and then out popped a plate with his name glowing green on it. "These are smart-plates, as silly as that is. The buffet table knows who each of us is. The assassin didn't need to poison the food, just the plates." Aegenor nodded, "So is yours poisoned?"

Aladdin whipped out a poison test strip and touched it to the plate. "Very much so, yes."

"Then what's in common between you and Cleopatra Hypercube?"

Aladdin shook his head. "Absolutely nothing except for..." Well, actually it was obvious and he shouldn't have even started that sentence. "She and I were both at the Librarian's meeting negotiating the treaties between the Rimward Orgs."

"So the Council is trying to take out the representatives?"

"Looks like. That'd be my guess."

Aegenor thought for a moment. "It's a long shot, but you can always see if the perpetrators left something behind inside the machine. They had to have installed something to poison the plates, after all. They didn't think they'd be caught yet, they might have not cleaned up yet, or done it sloppy."

"A fair point." He pulled out a screwdriver, which seemed like a weird thing to carry around, and began unscrewing the panel on the side of the buffet. "They probably just put in some sort of dispenser tied to the personal plate recognition." He popped the panel open, and the expression on Aladdin's face made it unquestionable that Aegenor would lean over to see what he was staring at.

It was quite the sight.

It was like nothing she had ever seen before.

Aegenor had heard of aliens, and she had seen Council aliens and Citlal, but somehow they still looked... relatable. They had one head, they had torsos and arms, and they had eyes and something resembling a face. What Aladdin was looking at did not have these qualities.

It was a long, matte dark grey, segmented rope. Its segments were pseudo cylindrical shells about the size of a soda can with black, rubbery looking flesh in the gaps. The armored segments each sprouted translucent blue tendrils and spines—some more rigid and some looser like tentacles, but all needle thin. There didn't seem to be a pattern to which were hard and which were soft. The texture of the segments was hard and rough, like worn-down sandpaper on top of a rock. The rope seemed to branch randomly, so that it wasn't a snake, and if you laid it out flat it would resemble neither a tree nor a stick figure. But at the end of each branch was a black talon, curved downward and sharp. There was a thin trench between the talon and the shell around it, and Aegenor had the odd impression that it was looking at the two of them from the gap, like the ring of an eye.

So that was that.

The next few seconds seemed to happen even faster than they did literally. One moment, Aladdin and the thing were having a mutually shocked staring contest, the next he was lunging, the next he had his hands around it, and the next it lurched back quickly –very quickly – because the next moment Aladdin wasn't there.

"Aladdin!" Aegenor yelled and rushed up to the hole, where she could see a long tunnel that a series of rails was moving dishes through, going down into the floor. Well, now was no time for waiting. Aegenor jumped in as well. The rails pulled her down into the machinery, and she could see Aladdin ahead of her. The thing was wrapped around his torso, and Aladdin was slamming its whipping tendrils into the machinery as it pulled them down...and then it started pulling them up. Aegenor slowly moved forward along the track that was pulling her, the gears ripping her dress as she squirmed. She just hoped this thing didn't narrow, or Aladdin and she were both dead. Pretty soon she could see Aladdin's feet, and then something strange happened. The thing latched onto Aladdin' spine. Aladdin looked surprised, but whatever the thing was doing, it didn't work out, because it began thrashing violently, as though it had thought it was dipping its foot into a calm pool of water only to find it was acid. Aegenor got closer to it, and as it thrashed she started beating the thing relentlessly, smashing it with her fists hard enough that she started cracking bit of its exoskeleton. This only made it thrash harder, and the spines on its body gashed her and Aladdin, but not before the ceiling beneath them came loose.

They had, in their little adventure, gone under the floor and along it, up the wall, and into the ceiling. When the ceiling broke, they tumbled down onto the floor, the strange creature falling in a mass of broken coils, writhing and shivering, squirming and thrashing. Aladdin and Aegenor staggered up, and drew their guns. Aegenor's being a bit harder to get out from the garter holster under her dress. If there was any time to unload a gun into something it was then, and they did so.

Aladdin panted and wiped his brow.

"I guess we solved the mystery."

"I think I hate mysteries."

Aladdin laughed in between breaths. At least this day couldn't get any weirder.

Research Sketch: Aegenor Valor

-A violent, angry young woman.

-Admires people who have gotten where they are without any help or assistance.

-Harder to get a trail on, as she has so little official documentation.

-Good at beating people up.

-Has a very serious personality.

-Likes cargo-vests and pants.

FILE 7:
ANYA HYPERCUBE'S DAY OUT

Anya was grinning pretty sneakily. Her face would light up, and she'd bite her lip smiling and then straighten her face out, because everything was totally normal. Ulysses knew better, of course. He was, after all, her brother..well, stepbrother...well, brother. "There something you want to tell me about that arm of yours, sis?"

Anya quit hiding her grin. "Aw, you noticed."

"Looks like you got some work done. Anything special?"

"This arm has bladed nails in it. They're super effective!" She flicked her hand, and out slid some lovely metal fingernails that could quite easily remove a person from being alive.

"Shiny. That's quite the slash you've got up in your arm. You're becoming a Pokémon."

"An-Anya," she said in her best anime voice.

"Does mom know?" Ulysses paused, and rephrased. "Does mom care?"

Being a member of the Hypercube family meant a lot of things. It meant that you had more siblings than most people had extended family (a grand total of fourteen children, from mid-20s to 6 years old), it meant you lived in a dome city on a space station in a manor house that wasn't kept at all clean, it meant that you were heirs to one of the larger shipping companies in the rim, and it meant that you were always wondering if your youngest sibling was always going to be your youngest sibling. Twelve of the kids were from the marriage of Michelangelo Hypercube and Geraldine "Jackbox" McGraw, but the oldest two were not. Anya was Michelangelo's kid from a previous relationship, and Ulysses was Geraldine's from her own. Anya was blonde and could pass for Geraldine's daughter if it came to it.. Though Geraldine had light brown hair, most of her children were blonde—just not quite as blonde as Anya. Ulysses, on the other hand, wasn't fooling anybody. He was half Korean, and boy did it show.

"Yeah, she knows."

"I don't know much about fashion, but they seem stylish."

"Geraldine seemed pleased. And hey, they'll come in handy if we run into trouble again!"

Ulysses leaned back in his chair and laughed. "They will, and knowing us, that's bound to happen."

Anya swung her hand through the air as though it was an enemy. It was effective against the air, but also shredded the curtain behind it.

"Anya! We just bought those. I think."

She shrugged. "Dad can get new ones. You know, Ulysses, there's so much out there to do. You and me, we should go out there and be big damn heroes. We could be that."

"That we could. I mean, what's stopping us? You can fix things, kill curtains you should probably be more worried about destroying, you're a good pilot, and I can beat up anyone who messes with you. Flawless team."

"You think I'm good at piloting? That means a lot to me."

Ulysses remembered dragging her out of the burning speeder, her arm and leg just bloody stumps of pulp... "I've never gotten a scratch on me when we fly."

"I've gotten better since the accident. Thank you."

"I know you have." He tousled her hair, and she laughed and shoved him playfully, then ran her fingers through her long hair to fix it.

"You know, we're just passing the time right now, but we don't have to be. We could go somewhere."

That was what Anya had been waiting to hear. Her eyes lit up with the promise of adventure.

"Well, where haven't we been to?"

"Never broke into a high class affair before, or met Dale Dinosaur Davis—"

"Oooooh! High class stuff. Think we can get away with it?"

"What's the worst that happens if we fail? We don't get invited back?"

"Geraldine told me some things about diplomats from the Index...they sounded like monsters."

"What exactly did they do?"

"She generalized. Said Dad wouldn't like it if she said too much. Said they were vicious psychos all jostling for a scrap of power, lying and cheating...the word treason came up a lot."

"Mom doesn't throw that word around lightly...I

wonder why she let Cleo go to that Index gala."

Anya stopped, her entire body frozen like Ulysses was a Gorgon.

"What do you mean our sister Cleopatra is meeting with them?"

Ulysses had thought she knew.

* * * * *

The two of them rode through the strange night of the dome city. It was entirely an artificial construct, one that many of the Titan's inhabitants thought should have been discarded decades ago. The great hot lights attached to the dome's ceiling were dimmed to weird pseudo darkness with just enough light to see, and the stars were thick above Anya's and Ulysses' heads. She had her hair down, and it flowed behind her in the wind. She was wearing her stepmom's dress, carefully pilfered from her closet. It was like something out of the 1920s, and jade green. It didn't look like Geraldine wore it much, so she figured it wouldn't be missed. Ulysses was wearing one of his stepdad's many tuxes. Even though they weren't related to their stepparents, they sized right. It pleased Ulysses to be like Michelangelo, and it made Anya feel slightly uncomfortable – though she would never admit it – to be so like Geraldine.

Their speeder closed in on the convention hall, a fat and boring block of a building with ornate sides, to hide the fact that it was essentially a brick, and a spire of a tower springing out of it. There was plenty of gold filigree on the place, and in front was the largest fountain Anya or Ulysses had ever seen shooting a geyser of water up towards the roof of the dome. There were vehicles of all shapes and sizes in front of it, including spaceships on their landing pads. All of them were clearly remarkably expensive. There was one thing that wasn't there, however.

"Where is the security? I was expecting...a lot, not none." Noises came from inside—loud ones. Anya looked at Ulysses. "That doesn't sound good. I knew this would be bad. Cleo has to be in trouble." Anya did what she wasn't supposed to do above all: speed. She tore through the parking lot, pulled up in front of the center and hopped over the door instead of opening it (which didn't quite work as she intended...she'd have to practice that), then barreled through the open doors into the building with Ulysses close behind.

What they saw when they got into the hall was not what they expected. The security wasn't outside because they were all in here, corralling hundreds of very finely dressed people, including one who stood out to Anya above all others. "Cleo!"

Her sister was crying, her makeup utterly ruined, her arms folded in front of her. Anya wasn't surprised that no one at the Index event was trying to help her. Cleo looked up and caught sight of her sister and brother, relief flooding her face. Ulysses tapped Anya on the shoulder and pointed at what Anya hadn't noticed at first glance, which was frankly embarrassing.

There on the floor was a large part of the ceiling. Amidst the rubble was a Martian kid, mid to late teens, and a Rimward girl of about the same age. The Martian boy was dressed in a very dirty tux, and was throwing off his glasses, which he didn't seem to need anyway. The girl was dressed in an evening gown she looked entirely uncomfortable in, which was even more torn and dirty then the boy's tux, on account of it being a dress. They were both holding guns. The really notable part, though, was the twitching, coiled thing on the floor that was clearly not of this world, or this solar system. It writhed and made strange sounds until the Martian boy and Rimward girl, stumbling, pulled out guns and shot the thing until it stopped quivering.

"Maybe it's our kind of party after all," Anya mused.

The Martian boy began stumbling over to a dark haired woman, and had a few words with her before sitting down in a chair and slumping over.

"Anya! Ule!"

They both turned, and Cleo rushed them with a teary hug. "Cleo!"

"Oh my gosh, I'm so glad you're both here! I know mom said she never wanted you to show up to this ever or something, but I couldn't be happier." She hugged them both again. "It was so awful, they poisoned me, and Aladdin and Aegenor got it out of me, but they couldn't save the Valkyrie girl, and then they went looking for the killer, and then they fell from the ceiling with the whatever that is, and I am just so so glad you're here!" she said very fast.

Anya tried to think of what to say. That was quite the burst of words, and as far as she could tell there was something rather seriously amiss at the moment.

"Why would they poison the food? Who poisoned it? Who are Aladdin and Aegenor?" Anya spat out, almost in an effort to not forget what she was wondering.

"I have no idea but Aladdin is over there," she pointed to the Martian boy who was rubbing his temples in a wingback chair.

"You should go talk to him, Anya."

"You're the diplomat of the family—" She protested

and turned to face Ulysses, who had Cleo wrapped up in a hug, or maybe buried was a better description. Ulysses looked at her with a face that fully expressed how little he could break out of this hold. Anya just gave him a thumbs up and started walking away, towards the Martian boy. She wasn't particularly adept at these sorts of things, but she'd certainly do her best. Of course, fate intervened to create a scenario far stranger than she ever intended.

When she walked up to Aladdin, she thought of how she could introduce herself to him. Break the ice, so to speak. She decided referencing a classic might work.

"Um...hey. So...mighty fine shindig ain't it?" Anya sputtered.

The Martian boy looked up from rubbing his eyes, and at first simply stared. The staring made Anya pretty uncomfortable.

"Do you know her?" The girl in the torn up dress asked the boy.

"How did you..." He reached for his pocket. She was pretty sure there was a gun in his pocket.

"How did I what?"

"You can't be real! You're dead! You died!" He reached his hand out towards her, shaking. She had no idea what was going on, and wasn't sure how this day could get any weirder. She gently reached out to touch his hand and show him she was real. He flinched as she did so.

"I... I don't know who you think I am, but I'm not her I'm definitely not dead, and I never have been."

"I'd know you anywhere. How did you get a new body? You think you can just...come back into my life and torture me again? I'm better then you, Jade Darkshadow! I know your face. How could I forget it? You look younger, though."

Anya had heard that name before, way too many times, from other strangers thinking she was this Jade Darkshadow. Anya was annoyed he'd mistaken her for her as well, but whoever this Jade was, she was clearly a jerk, and clearly nothing like Anya.

"Um….I'm Anya Hypercube. That's my name. Are you Jhe Aladdin?"

If his face had been one of anger and shock before, his new one was that of shock, confusion and embarrassment, and maybe still anger.

"...Anya Hypercube? You're Anya Hypercube...YOU'RE...Anya...oh dear. I'm Jhe Aladdin. Um...hi." They shook hands awkwardly.

"You know me? Of me?"

"I know someone...like you. And your sister mentioned that I reminded her of you in some weird way."

"Oh...well, I came to ask if you knew why someone would poison the food. Or what that thing was, or why someone would want to hurt Cleo."

"I'll answer yours if you answer mine."

"Okay?"

"The food was poisoned because The Emperors of the Council are trying to destroy the trade agreement between the Rim Orgs. They tried to take out all of the representatives of each of the Rim Orgs tonight with his..."

The girl, who must be Aegenor, cut in. "I think it's a spy."

"You call that a spy?"

"It talked!"

"You call that talking?"

"Shut the hell up!"

"You—anyways, the spy didn't exactly work out..."

"Because we shot it"

"Yes we did. So the answer is The Emperors and their henchmen poisoned the food."

Anya was horrified. The horror showed on her face. "Why would he want to do that?"

"They're fighting a war, and they want to break our backs so they can take over our solar system...well, our reality. You heard about the war on Earth? What he's been doing there? He's not stopping there."

The look of horror on her face increased tenfold and Aladdin realized he'd just overloaded her. "Sorry, do you need to sit down? We have chairs...I just killed an eldritch horror from beyond creation—"

"We killed," Aegenor cut in.

"Yes, we killed—so trust me I know the feeling."

Anya sat down. She would have asked for a drink, but her sister had just been poisoned, so no. "So The Emperors and the Council want to take over the solar system as well as our whole plane of existence, and they want to do that by killing some Rim representatives?"

"Yes, they do, and this one action wouldn't win the war, but it would cause a lot of chaos in our ranks. They did only send one..." Aladdin looked at the corpse of the alien, "...guy?"

"So The Emperors almost killed my sister."

"Yes they did. Their failure was accidental."

Anya was angry. Angrier than she had ever felt before, angrier than she knew she could feel. She was shaking. Her fists clenched, the metal one squeaking a bit as she strained the motors in it.

Aladdin's eyes were like moons. He looked like a child realizing his parent was getting into "that mood" again.

"I-It's okay. It's gunna be okay. Y-y-you don't h-h-have to get angry. She's okay."

Aegenor shoved Aladdin aside. "Shut up, of course she's angry, I'd wanna kill the bastard too after this." Aladdin just put his hands in his pockets and looked away. "You good? You wanna yell or break something?"

It was a high class establishment, which made it that much more rewarding when Aegenor picked up a chair, holding it out to Anya, and Anya took it from her and smashed it to bits on the ground like a rock star who got the wrong color M&Ms. Aladdin just walked away.

"Feel better?"

"Lots. Sorry, just, we're a close family, the Hypercubes, and it makes me very angry when people threaten any of my siblings, or my dad for that matter...or my stepmom. We're really loyal."

Aegenor smiled with sad envy. Across the room, Cleo and Ulysses were looking much happier and Ulysses was still doing things to cheer his sister up, which only multiplied the burning envy inside Aegenor's heart.

"Must be nice, a family like that. Sorry about Aladdin, he's a little punk. I don't know why he's freaking out at you so much. Looks like he saw a ghost or something. Dude is such a spazz."

"It's okay. I wish I knew what was bugging him."

"He's really not Index material."

"Aw damn, Dad is going to be so pissed when he finds out about this!"

"Why?"

"His daughter was almost murdered."

"Oh yeah."

"And I'm not supposed to be here."

"...Why?"

"My dad and Geraldine always get super weird whenever the Index is involved in anything. They didn't even tell me they were sending Cleo here. They're also weird about the Spinneret, but none of the other Rimward groups. I wish they'd just...talk to me."

Aegenor bit her lip. "Aladdin's dad runs the Spinneret you know. You could ask him."

"He's acting weird."

"I wouldn't know."

"But you're here with him."

"I'm not his date, just his assigned escort."

Anya suddenly stopped and realized she had skipped over an important piece of information. "Wait a second—you said his dad runs the Spinneret?!"

* * * * *

Anya had never seen a fountain so big. The geyser in the center was huge, nearly the height of the habitation dome. It was plastered with signs that clearly said not to climb it or throw things in it. Aladdin had scaled the "No climbing!" ledge and stood, hands in his pockets, watching the water move. She walked up slowly.

"Aladdin?"

"Come on up."

She climbed clumsily, trying not to tear her stepmom's dress, and Aladdin reached down a shaky hand to pull her up.

"Thanks." She stood on the ledge next to him and dusted the dress off. The view here on the fountain was beautiful, rainbows arcing through the tub of the fountain among huge streams of water and the hot illuminating lights.

"Welcome...I'm sorry about earlier. You make me rather uncomfortable, nothing about you..."

"Something to do with Jade Darkshadow?"

"A lot to do with Jade Darkshadow. What's that mean to you?"

"Nothing, just heard you say it earlier. Who is she?"

"She is a woman my father knew a long time ago. She's dead. The Librarian killed her two decades ago. But I've known her my whole life."

Anya could not have been more confused by that sentence."What?"

"Sorry, it's weird. Weird is definitely the right word. Do you believe in souls?"

"Yeah? I guess. I haven't really spent a lot of time pondering it.'"

"My father and Jade Darkshadow did some sort of...experiment. I'm still fuzzy on a lot of it. But their souls got linked together and when she died...her consciousness lingered. What happened wasn't supposed to, and so when she died she was still tethered here somehow. When I was growing up, she would talk to me, enter my dreams... Sorry, you must think I'm crazy. You should go. I shouldn't have said anything."

"No, this is interesting. Their souls linked? How is that possible? And what kinds of things did she say to you in your dreams?"

"I don't know how it is. No one has been able to replicate it. It was a freak accident. When she visited me in my dreams, she told me about her life, or told me what she dreamed I would become. She built empires of thought and treated me like a beloved son, and then when I made her angry she beat me and hurt me and left me alone for a year locked in my dreams. I was her toy, and her tool, and I think she wanted to use me for her goals she never achieved in life. And then she just...disappeared."

"Wha... That's horrible. She mentally abused you, and then abandoned you out of nowhere?"

"You've got the gist of it. You're taking this pretty well. This isn't exactly normal stuff."

She shrugged. Anya had experienced some bad things in her time, like when she'd crashed her speeder and seen her arm and leg in bloody chunks next to her, but she had been an adult then.

"Your dad knew her? Aegenor said he ran the Spinneret."

He nodded. "Yeah, he knew her. You've probably heard of my dad, he goes by the name Kalingkata usually."

Anya had heard of Kalingkata, the famous Rimward hacker who ran the Spinneret, who fought the Council, and won a Nobel Prize for science.

"Wow. Yeah, I've heard of him. He's pretty famous huh?"

"Yeah, he probably helped design something in that arm of yours."

She grinned. "This isn't a traditional arm, I modded it pretty heavily."

Aladdin smiled, finally. "I can tell. You've done some good work on it." Not to mention the robotic parts made her look less like Jade. "Anything notable you did to it?"

"Promise you won't freak out?"

"I just told you ghosts are real and you look exactly like a dead woman who haunted me since I was a baby. I think we are past that point."

She flicked out the bladed nails from her hand, and Aladdin leaned in to inspect them. They were really a work of art—some Rimward craftsman had done a great job with them. "Careful, they're sharp!"

He laughed. "I can see that. Monomolecular edge?"

"You bet!"

"I'd high five you, but I still need this hand."

She slid her nails in, and the two of them performed said gesture, framed by a burst from the fountain.

"You're quite the mystery woman, Anya Hypercube. I take it your parents are the famous Michelangelo and Geraldine Hypercube of the Cube2Hypergang?"

"Yep! I mean, well, sort of. My dad is Michelangelo, Geraldine is my stepmom."

Aladdin raised an eyebrow. "Oh? Well, is it rude to ask who your birth mother was?"

Anya turned away from him and looked at the water rise. "I...don't know. I asked Dad, and he told me it was something he didn't want to talk about."

"I'm sorry, really sorry. That must be hard for you."

"It is." She kept staring.

Aladdin thought for a moment, and touched her on the shoulder. As Anya turned to look at him, he withdrew an orange from his bag. Anya tilted her head to the side, and then Aladdin pointed to a sign,

"DO NOT THROW ANYTHING INTO THE FOUNTAIN."

Aladdin held the orange out to her, and made a mock throwing motion. Anya smiled at him faintly, took the orange, and chucked it at the fountain with all the force her cybernetic arm could muster, which was plenty. The orange shot up the towering geyser in the center of the fountain and then kept going up. However, there is only so much up in a city dome, and the orange exploded into droplets against the clear dome, the bits of orange reflecting the starlight like a cold firework. Anya laughed and spun in a circle, watching the shining orange droplets. Aladdin was pleased. "That's better. I didn't mean to make you sad."

"It's okay, I like getting to talk about it, really. I'm not the only one with that problem in my family. Ulysses is Geraldine's kid, and she won't tell him who his dad is. I think he's from a previous marriage."

"Was he the one hugging Cleo?"

"Yep. He looks a little like you to be honest."

"Korean ancestry in his genes, pretty clearly... You really do look a lot like Jade Darkshadow to be honest."

She sighed, and he could tell he shouldn't have made the comparison again. She looked tired as soon as it came out of his lips. "Yeah, but that's about all we know. They've really kept a lot of secrets from us."

"Same here. My dad didn't tell me about Jade. I had to find out on my own."

"People do keep calling me Darkshadow on accident. I hate all these mysteries."

"What do you imagine your mom like?" He tilted the conversation.

"I don't know. I've imagined her in lots of different ways over the years, as basically everything a mother could be. She could have been anyone. And there are plenty of reasons Dad wouldn't want to talk about her. Maybe he was in love with her and she died tragically...or she's stuck out there and something is keeping her from being able to see us. I've imagined any possible reason she has never been a part of my life. Sometimes she's a great hero, defending far-off places. Sometimes she's trapped in an alien jail in a different system. Sometimes she's a Companion, like Inara in Firefly. You've seen that right?"

"I studied the classics."

"I have a wild imagination. It provides a lot of

possibilities."

"You do have a great imagination. I hope you find her someday." Actually, he didn't. He was pretty damn sure he knew who her mom was. And if he was right, she didn't want to know.

"Thank you. I should get back to my family, Ulysses and Cleo must be wondering where I am."

Aladdin nodded, and the two of them hugged. It seemed only appropriate. Aladdin had never expected to meet this girl, had never expected her to exist, and most of all had never expected to like her.

"I'm glad I met you, Anya Hypercube."

"I'm glad I met you, Jhe Aladdin."

"One last thing." Aladdin reached into his bag and pulled out two more oranges. Anya grinned like, just for this moment, the stars shined just for her.

The cleaning crew the next morning was not pleased.

* * * * *

"Well that was an interesting report."

"I thought you'd want to know about this part immediately," I told you as you sat in your handcrafted Italian chair. You were drinking a cappuccino. Elegantly.

"I think I'll assign Aladdin to their protection. Jack Zeus shouldn't mind too much. He'll probably think I'm just vying for a favorable rate on the next deal with the Olympians."

"Well I'm glad you're being so kind."

You looked up from the data pad. "I never said I wouldn't use this to get a better shipping rate. I just hadn't planned it till now."

Of course, should have figured that.

"Tell the Hypercubes Jhe Aladdin will be coming to stay to prevent any further attacks, and get other agents to cover the other people at the Gala. But I think that whoever is doing this is following a trail. I don't think this is about what it appears."

I raised an eyebrow, but you were and are the Boss. I just hoped the Hypercubes would be receptive.

DEEP BACKGROUND: BACKGAMMON JENNY

Getting the dirt on the illusive, elusive, Backgammon Jenny was very very difficult. Parts are easy, everyone knows she was an orphan that Jhe Sang Ki paid for the education of. That's practically advertised as the Spinneret's official sap story. But what did she do between the orphanage and trying to kill you and Sang Ki?

From the sources I've talked to, she went on a quest to find someone to train her. Who that ended up being though, I have no idea. I like to imagine her on a mountain top with some martial arts teacher spouting pithy but stoic quips about life and training.

Where she trained is also a mystery. She dropped off the face of the universe. But I suppose in the end the details of the answers aren't that important so much as the broad strokes.

Research Sketch:
Anya Hypercube

-The eldest child of Michelangelo Hypercube.
-Good with technology.
-On good terms with her stepmother, Geraldine "JackBox" Hypercube née McGraw.
-Has an adventurous, sometimes reckless, personality.
-Like putting steampunk ornamentation on her mechanical limbs.

FILE 8:
MEMNORIC DEVICES

Memnor was born under a set of stars you can't even see from the skies of earth. So far away was the orb of rock, that when the Great Assimilation stumbled upon the world Memnor was spawned on, they barely believed they had made it. The skies were filled with black, and the stars themselves were sparse. No moons rotated over the dark planet's skies, and its dim sun gave more warmth than daylight. When the outlines of The Three Emperors' cruisers began to block out the stars and the sun, Memnor stretched its tendril towards the sky. Unlike the rest of its kind, which reeled in confusion (an emotion that passed for terror in that world), it realized this was its chance. They crawled out of their holes to stare at the sky, as Memnor crawled back down and began to plot.

When Admiral Moloch of the Council landed, Memnor was ready. The others were overwhelmed as Moloch and The Three Emperors walked over their soil and seemed to

project an aura of Godhood, but Memnor climbed a rock.
The others rose from their holes and coiled in deference at
the feet of the beings who walked over them. Memnor
crested the rock, and rapped a long, curved talon against
it. The male Emperor looked at Memnor and raised an
eyebrow, and Memnor focused as hard as it could to
project a thought into the man's mind. The Emperor
pushed the thought away, and pushed back. Memnor felt
its neural pathways overload with his mind, and it
prostrated itself before him. But Memnor had made its
point. When The Emperors gathered Memnor's race
together for their operations on other worlds, they
appointed Memnor to be in charge.

Memnor soon organized its people into something
they were good at: information gathering. They could rip
out the memories of most other races by forcibly digging
into their nervous systems and 'hacking in,' as The
Emperors called it. Soon, Memnor had to grow new
segments to store all the memories it was collecting.
Before The Emperor's armadas besieged a world, Memnor
would drop down an operative, and it would slither and
slink to find some unsuspecting being and jam into its
nervous system. Sometimes, depending on the species,
they had to be carved up a bit before that could happen.
Memnor loved getting the new memories transferred. It
would spend hours figuring out each new species' thought
patterns, and then collect more memories. Memnor held
not only its own, but also the collected wisdom of
thousands of lives. Knowledge was power, and Memnor
sought to be the most powerful it could.

But Memnor couldn't meet its true potential, because there would be an end to Memnor's life. Sure, it could transfer its memories to another of its kind, but that creature would not be Memnor. But as Memnor rose through the ranks and became more important, it learned that there was another path. As Memnor began to steal the memories of important beings within The Emperor's Government, some called it the Council, some the Great Assimilation, it learned that The Emperors were not limited by one body. This was a moment of epiphany for Memnor, for Memnor knew that The Emperors were indeed Gods then, and Memnor knew that Godhood was not out of reach for itself, either. The question was not if, but how, and Memnor began the search. After some targeted assassinations, subtle blackmailing and that sort of thing, Memnor reached its place on the Council. Coiled with pride at its new seat, Memnor hoped to learn information it had been longing to learn for years... information the Council was blind to. Information the Council was ignorant to.

It soon became clear that the Council were morons, and Memnor's ambitions, intelligence, and knowledge outdid all of them. When The Emperors began their campaign into the Sol system of what the called the Prime reality, not the same Universe Memnor had been born into by a longshot, Memnor leaped at the chance to leave the dusty chambers of the Council and get back into the field. But of course, it mostly just sent its operatives and let them bring memories back to it. That is, until one of its operatives brought back something worth Memnor's personal attention.

"Who is this being?" Memnor said by touching one of its thin spines to one of its operative's spines and jolting electricity into it—their kind's normal way of communicating.

"It used to work with this universe's most notable beings. It has memories of...practices of interest."

Memnor perceived the being and analyzed its physical characteristics. "The being is a 'he,' like the male Emperor. It is a primarily binary-sex species, though there seem to be many exceptions. I am still studying that."

"This one, he, calls itself Amaterasu."

"Where did you find it?"

"It was sniping our soldiers on Earth."

"Its markings show it as Martian."

"It appears to have gone rogue. If you examine its memories you will find its reasoning."

"His reasoning."

"Sorry, his reasoning."

"Transfer me his memories."

"I think you will want to look at its memories in person."

Memnor did not need to question its subordinate. It knew its place, and it knew if something was important enough to dare tell Memnor to do it. The Martian man pursed his lips and expelled liquid on Memnor, the saliva from his mouth dripping off its exoskeleton. A strange reaction. Memnor slithered to the back of the chair the man was tied to, and moved up his spine. Maybe Memnor would understand why he spit when it jacked into his brain? Its spines dug into his spine, and Ameratsu's eyes looked like he wanted to scream louder than he ever had, but there was no noise, only silence.

* * * * *

"Earth is being ravaged—there aren't going to be people left there by the time the Council's done!"

"Colonel, calm down. You may be in charge of the Special Forces division, but that doesn't mean you can make the decisions around here." The General was smoking, which struck Amaterasu as the kind of needless excess you could get away with when you had a desk job and didn't need to keep your body at its finest to make sure the men and women serving under you didn't die.

"It means I should get a say."

"No, it doesn't."

Amaterasu grimaced, saluted, and walked out.

"How'd it go?" Kitsune asked him, hiding a flask in her jacket.

"Bad. Tell the unit we're going to Earth, General Xi be damned."

"Are you serious? We'll be court martialed."

"We don't exist. Try court martialing two decades of nonexistent black ops missions. The Government can deal with this."

Soon Amaterasu and the best snipers and assassins on Mars were on an unmarked ex-Centro stealth ship heading for Earth. They got through the blockade and—

"Enough, let's go back earlier."

Amaterasu looked over at the robed thing, coiled, dark and silent.

"Who are you?"

"I'm no one. Now let's go back in time."

* * * * *

"This will work," Kalingkata said. "I'll just hop into your brain, and we can hack the this tech through your mental powers."

Jade Darkshadow looked reluctant, but he talked her into it. They lay down on the ground, a device around Kalingkata's head, a transceiver plugged into the data jack that linked to Jade's brain. She was a telepath, could communicate with her mind, and the enemy they were facing that day used technology that linked with minds to run. Faceless beings from another dimension, with strange crystal ships. The link worked, and Amaterasu watched as Kalinkata shut down or took control of the enemy ship they had boarded. They were in control. It was all so simple.

"They did it, I can't believe it," Amaterasu muttered under his breath. Fei, their doctor, examined the pair closely. "They're both stable. Can you hear me Jade?"

The body nodded.

"We need to separate you. Now, all you have to do is pull the transceiver out. I can't do it for you, since you locked your brain access port to your bespoke biosignature. So reach up, very carefully, and pull it out slowly. Don't rush. You don't want to mess this up."

Jade's hand reached up. Her fingers closed on the device.

Everyone held their breath, Amaterasu remembered the silence.

When Jade broke the transceiver and Kalingkata was stuck in her brain, Memnor knew it had found God.

"This is it, thank you Amaterasu. This is it."

Amaterasu didn't remember that voice. It was out of place...it was...

Memnor slid its tendrils out of his spine, and addressed its operative, "We must keep this meeting secret, do you understand?"

"I do, Councilor Memnor."

"Excellent. I will erase any memories this one had of you or me or this meeting, and you will put him back with his unit. You will also give him data on our troop movements, and I'll give him a memory of leaving camp to stalk one of our soldiers and get the info out of it."

"They are snipers. They will slaughter the whole unit we inform them of."

"The losses are necessary. I am on the cusp of something important. Something larger then this war. He must have no suspicions this occurred. No one must wonder where he went."

"I understand, Councilor."

Memnor, if it could smile, would have. The secret to being immortal, to shifting bodies, was no longer The Emperors' alone. It was in this Kalingkata and this Jade, too.

It would need to research...

* * * * *

The interrogations were long, and spanned worlds. It found out secrets even the people who were involved in the secrets didn't know. It found out lies and treachery. And it found out that Jade was dead, but not dead, and that Kalingkata and she were on the most heavily guarded ship in the universe. Memnor could not steal memories from there. It had tried, and it had failed. It raged in frustration until it learned more secrets, stealing them in the night with old fashioned archive searching. It had a list of names.

One of them was Jhe Aladdin, Kalingkata's son, who seemed tied to Jade somehow.

The rest of them all had the last name Hypercube.

And that made Memnor's job so much easier.

Research Sketch:
Memnor

-From another Solar System in another universe.

-The head of the Great Assimilation's (also called "The Council", a name based on its secondary governing body) intelligence agency.

-Has the natural ability to communicate with the nervous systems of other living beings.

-Creepy looking, honestly.

FILE 9:
FOUR CHESS GAMES

Two weeks earlier...

    You weren't usually puzzled by board games, ever. Leave it to your first-ever intern to confuse you. "Aladdin, dear, I don't understand this Chess variant. It doesn't make sense."

    "It does, you just have to realize what the point of playing the game is."

    You didn't reveal your frustration, just smiled sweetly. You had no idea what the point of all of this was, but Aladdin had brewed up some of the best tea you'd ever drunk, and you knew you'd play some regular chess after you finished the five games of this you'd promised him. You were at least enjoying yourself, as much as you ever enjoyed yourself, but that didn't change the fact that this was one of the oddest Chess variants you had ever played. You'd think it was just poorly made if Aladdin didn't have a fully written out rule set and wasn't musing about strategy the whole time.

Aladdin took her rook. "Viva!"

"Viva," you muttered. "Aladdin dear, let's play something else?"

He nodded. You were his boss, after all. He looked out the window at the stars, musing that somewhere out there was a much better person to play Red Breaker Chess with. He should know. He'd played them.

Two and a half years earlier...

Aladdin and Greed debated loudly about which one of them had invented Red Breaker Chess, but the truth was they had created together when they were kids. Greed's dad had accidently destroyed some of the pieces on their chessboard, leaving gaping holes in their military lines. It was clear the game wouldn't be fair, as it was pretty much guaranteed black would win, so they forged a new game with the following rules:

-Players only get one of every non-pawn piece. Each one of those pieces may be placed in either of the two spots one could be for that player.

-All empty squares are to be filled with metal slugs (you can use other things, but if you use credit chips expect them to be stolen) which all count as pawns.

-The king has a special ability that can be used no more than twice per game per king. This ability allows the king to move as though he were a queen for that turn, though if the player chooses he may also move the King as though he were a knight. When this ability is activated all pawns for both players permanently may move an extra square. This stacks every time the ability is used, to a maximum of 5 squares of movement.

-If there are no pieces left aside from pawns (and pieces pawns transformed into) and kings, both players lose and the pawns hold a revolution and overthrow the monarchy.

Aladdin and Greed had become masters of this game, though most other people thought it was silly.

"The game doesn't work, you made it too easy for both players to lose and the pawns to win their Revolution." Lalita Mashima, the daughter of the President, had said one day when Greed had visited Mars, and the three of them had spent the day slumming around cafes.

"That's the point." Greed said, as though Lalita had tried to point out that the problem with peanut butter was that it tasted like peanut butter.

"It doesn't make much game sense though. You both lose the game half the time."

Aladdin moved his metal slug forward three spaces, "It doesn't have to. We made the game for ourselves to play, we're not going to sell it on Earth or anything. If we have fun both losing, isn't that good enough?"

Lalita looked at the board as Greed made his next move, and sipped her cappuccino. "I just don't get it. It's a stupid game Aladdin, and a bad one." Aladdin shrugged, he doubted he'd ever find someone who understood why Greed and he had made the game this way.

Two-ish years later...

"Oh my God this is the greatest game I've ever played in my life!" Nightingale started setting up the board again without even asking if Aladdin wanted to play again; he was really tired.

"I'm glad you're enjoying i-"

"It's so brilliant! I want to lose every time! And it's in

the rules there's a revolution and they kill the kings or send them to deserted islands or whatever, and the people are free and we need to play again." Nightingale looked happier than he'd seen her...practically ever. "Let's play again. You can go first."

Aladdin moved a pawn forward. Nightingale did the same. "You know, I don't think anyone has really appreciated this game outside of Greed and me before. Well, Backgammon Jenny I guess."
Nightingale looked up from her board examination. "You know someone named Backgammon Jenny?"

"She loves board games. Jenny's from the Rim."

"I'm not surprised."

"She works for my dad, she's his personal assistant, secretary...something. Basically she runs the Spinneret when he isn't there." Aladdin moved his bishop so Nightingale could slaughter it next turn, "I've known her since I was little because of that. I've always wondered why she went to work for my dad, or why he hired her."

"It's not too uncommon for people to get jobs. That is a normal part of most people's live you know." Nightingale chirped, as she destroyed centuries of government control of religion to aid in political subjugation with her pawn.

"I mean, they met when she went to go kill my dad. Apparently he told her something that changed her mind. Changed it so much she started working for him."

"That must have been one heckuva story."

Greed opened the door. "Dinner is in half an hour. Our game?"

"Yep."

"It's the best game ever," Nightingale added.

"See, Nightingale gets it. You should hit on her rather than that Lalita chick. Peace." He shut the door. There was a pregnant silence.

"So, Chess?" Aladdin said as he blushed.

"Lalita chick?"

"Old girlfriend."

Nightingale moved her knight into sacrifice position, and Aladdin proceeded to destroy the idolization of the military used to support inhumane social structures.

"How many people have even played this game?" Aladdin was so grateful for the change in subject.

"Not too many, though we did put the rules on the internet once. So maybe more than I think." Nightingale smiled, hoping someone else out there understood it like they did.

* * * * *

Anya and Ulysses Hypercube sat on the living room floor and stared at the board.

"This was our third game, and we've both lost every time."

Ulysses shook his head. "This is a weird game. I don't really get it."

"Neither do I." Anya went over to the game cabinet, "Let's play something else. Monopoly? Risk? Scrabble?"

"Eh?"

"Backgammon?"

"I could do that. That's the game with the Doubling Cube right?"

Anya grinned. "I always like to think of it as the Hypercube."

Carl Fredrickson

Research Sketch: Geraldine 'Jackbox' Hypercube

-Co-Owner of the Cube2Hypergang, which is primarily a shipping company.
-Wife of Michelangelo Hypercube, mother of too many children.
-Former associate/girlfriend of Kalingkata/Jhe Sang Ki.
-Came up from nothing, living on the streets, to being one of the most influential Rimward figures.
-Bowiest Christian

FILE 10:
A DESOLATION OF HYPERCUBES

Geraldine 'JackBox' Hypercube was mad as hell, and her husband was hearing all about it.

"NO! I am not having Jhe Aladdin in my house, Michelangelo! I refuse!"

"Well, he already met your son, and they seem to be getting along well." Geraldine glared at him like a Gorgon. "Geraldine, there is way too much at stake to not let the Librarian help us."

"Then have the Librarian send someone else!"

"You know that isn't how this works; the Librarian isn't going to just...let us appeal for different terms when they offer us help. The Index isn't that kind." Geraldine scowled. Michelangelo held her gaze, and the staring contest could have been professional.

Carl Fredrickson

"You know how much I don't want this. Anya and Ulysses might learn things from that boy. Things they can't unlearn."

He ran his fingers through his immaculate hair and sighed. "They might, they might not, but I won't leave our kids in unnecessary danger because you won't accept the Librarian's pet. The Council isn't a joke; they'll tear through us, one by one, like he tried to start with Cleopatra. Do you want to see Boudicca dead? Leonidas? Eowyn? Z-"

"I get it alright!" Geraldine walked over to the sink. The metal was polished so that she could see a blurry outline of herself in its basin. Turning the tap on, she watched the image jar further until her reflection was lost in the flow of water, which she sunk her hands into and splashed onto her face. Her shape dripped back into the basin.

"Fine," she said, as the water sunk down the drain. "I'll let you bring Jhe Aladdin here. But on your head be it."

* * * * *

Anya ran her metal hand through her hair, letting it blow back into the wind and into Beowulf's face. She was speeding, technically, which her mostly-twin Ulysses would frown on if he was here, but he wasn't. Her hair turned into streamers in the open speeder, declaring this road to be Hypercube territory. She grinned. Well, at least it was Anya Hypercube's territory.

"Can we slow down?" Kriemheld asked, hesitantly. Her hair was bound back in a bandanna, and she had to hold it on with her hands as the wind caught it like a sail.

"Do I have to?"

Kriemheld's response, which was to simply widen her eyes to the point that you might think she didn't have eyelids, was enough. With a sigh, Anya slowed the speeder down and puttered her way to the spaceport. Kriemheld was going through a phase of dressing super modestly, wearing layers of clothes and fingerless gloves, high collars and head coverings. Anya wasn't sure what was up with it, but considering how Rim folk usually dressed, it was downright weird. Beowulf was just glad his sister's hair wasn't in his face and that he had gotten out of being a wingman for Gilgamesh's date with his new boyfriend.

At the spaceport, Aladdin, dressed in a very nice pinstripe blue suit, was looking very intently at a computer on his arm. It spoke back to him with a voice as old as centuries, and Aladdin listened. A woman sat next to him with a made up name, and she just stared at her hand as she clenched and unclenched it, the mechanisms moving to pull the fingers, signals moving through connections, and she was unsure if she was flesh or machine. Far above all of them the stars moved, and dodged holes in reality, while fleets that dwarfed nations slaughtered and re-slaughtered each other in endless succession. This was the scene, this was the time, this was how Memnor had planned it, and this is how the desolation of Hypercubes would begin.

* * * * *

Aladdin waved at the speeder, and Anya smiled at him and swirled the speeder to a halt that was half joy channeled through driving, and half clear showing off. Aladdin smiled back, good to finally see a friendly face. Aegenor just kept silent and tilted her closed lips.

"Aladdin!"Anya yelled, stepping over the door as she speeder slowed its final few inches. Inside, two passengers who were clearly her younger siblings, very slowly unbuckled themselves.

"Anya, how've you been? I'm glad to have been assigned here."

Anya hugged him. "Don't sound so formal. You're about to live with the Hypercubes, and formality is forbidden by law."

"That's pretty extreme."

"When in Rome 2.0."

"Revolt?"

Anya was not expecting that answer. "Or, do like the Romans."

"Revolt still sounds better."

"I think you've had some weird influences."

"Only the best."

"Are you going to introduce us or what?" Beowulf was messing with a yo-yo, spinning it and pulling it up to bounce lightly against his brown leather jacket. Aladdin could make out what looked like a Carnival Reichenbach t-shirt under it. He'd heard that band before, but never really liked them.

"Oh, sorry! Jhe Aladdin, this is Beowulf Hypercube." Beowulf kind of limply shook Aladdin's hand. "Hey."

"Pleasure to meet you."

"Yeah."

"And this is my sister Kriemheld." Aladdin held out his hand, and she just sort of smiled and let his hand hang in the air. "Er, don't worry about her, she's going through a phase."

"So I see."

"It's not a phase, Anya."

"Fine, it's not a phase, just help Aladdin get his stuff in the car." They did, and as they loaded, there was a twitching in the shadows, like the last remnants of rigor mortis.

* * * * *

Geraldine 'JackBox' Hypercube knew her daughter was speeding, and she didn't care. She didn't care that it was dangerous, and she didn't care that she'd specifically told Anya not to do it not very long ago. Geraldine was too busy looking at the boy in the passenger seat, the boy who, if he took off his glasses, looked exactly like someone she'd tried very hard to forget.

"Mom, I can see them coming."

"Yes, Ule, I can to." She could see them singing something indistinguishable. She couldn't help but think of Nine Inch Nails; she couldn't help but think of looking over at a boy as his eyes focused on a circuit board, and how weird it was to feel her heart jump when she saw him make the connection in his head. She couldn't help but hate the boy in the car.

Anya pulled up, she'd mastered the technique of parking the car and walking over the door as it finished its final bit of deceleration by counting the pulses of the grav dampeners for timing, and she couldn't help but do it every time she parked the car. The boy opened the door like a normal person, and adjusted his glasses, which Geraldine could tell from a distance weren't for his eyesight, but wearable tech. It was super retro. What a fop, and very unlike his dad, at least.

"Welcome to the Hypercube household!" Michelangelo said, opening his muscular arms wide and taking in the vastness of the estate of the street urchins.

The boy's face bloomed into a smile. "Glad to be here. Jhe Aladdin."

Michelangelo shook his hand, Aladdin complimented him on something, wittily, and the strong man laughed. Geraldine didn't note what was said, she just stared at Aladdin.

"And this is my wife, Geraldine Hypercube," Michelangelo smiled at her, a pleading expression that spoke decades of, "I know," and years of, "I'm sorry."

"A pleasure," she said, and let his hand hang there like her daughter had. Aladdin was struck with the sudden impression that something in the X chromosomes of this family precluded hand shaking.

"Great! That went well," Michelangelo boomed.

It what? Aladdin thought.

"Now let me introduce you to my children, Anya, Ulysses, Zoroaster, Cleopatra, Leonidas, Hypatia, Gilgamesh, Beowulf, Kriemheld, Brunhild, Murasaki, Eowyn, Valentinez and Boudicca."

There was a moment of very comic pause before Aladdin said, "Can you repeat that a few times?"

It should be noted, for those readers curious, that Aladdin made a joke about the strength of Michelangelo's handshake and whether he gripped his paintbrushes that way. This holds no bearing to the plot, but we felt it should be noted regardless.

* * * * *

The Hypercube estate consists of one very large mansion, with more rooms then even a family with fourteen children knows what to do with, a swimming pool, tennis court and several statues that came with the mansion (much of the family is unsure what they are even depictions of) scattered across a large and largely unkempt lawn. The flowers and the vegetable garden are well tended, but after years of family members passing off who would mow the lawn, and a general agreement they shouldn't get servants to do it, they had to come up with another solution. The lawn gets taken care of so irregularly that to motivate everyone to both, the family takes great amusement in cutting down the prairie that's grown with swords, much to the consternation of the neighbors.

The estate also contains a second, much smaller, but very chic house. This was the house of the only person to complain about the Hypercube's messy household to the homeowners association. Geraldine and Michelangelo bought out the homeowners association, and then bought the home of the guy next door, who had always been creepy anyway. The mansion, being a mansion, has many nooks and crannies for private reading sessions—a feature Hypatia loves about her home, and that Leonidas uses to make out with his constant stream of boy and girlfriends. Beowulf has been trying to take after his older brother's example, but only with girls, and has found himself frustratingly shy.

There is also a racquetball court, a full size gymnasium, and a movie theater in the basement. Some days Michelangelo and Geraldine still wake up in their king size bed, look out the window at all that they own, and think that they must be dreaming, and that the nightmares they still have about the men who sold their bodies as children are the reality. Then the dawn sets in, and they realize that no—this is real, and this is good, and they will bite the throats out of anyone who tries to take this away from them.

* * * * *

"This will be your room, Aladdin." Anya sat down on the bed, and bounced up and down on it by rocking her heels. "It's a good room. It used to be Ulysses and mine before we got old enough we wanted separate ones."

Aladdin scanned the walls, which still held the pale rectangles from where posters had shielded the walls from fading. Aegenor looked around unimpressed, very unimpressed. "I'm honored to be staying here."

"Honor's a pretty Martian word. I thought you were Europan. Or at least Index." Ulysses noted, or asked.

"My dad runs the Spinneret," he responded.

"That.... doesn't actually explain that."

"My dad's from Mars."

"Gotcha. Hey, so's mine."

Anya laughed, "oh yeah, you two have so much in common. You can switch jobs tomorrow. Aladdin can do the lifting, Ulysses can do the hacking."

"I'm more than just a bunch of muscle you know."

She stuck her tongue out. She knew.

"I'm... definitely not a bunch of muscle," Aladdin said.

Anya looked between her brother and Aladdin. She could see a resemblance, but it was just that they both had Korean Martian in them. It really was unfair to think otherwise. After all, she apparently looked like that Jade Darkshadow lady, but she wasn't related to her.

Aegenor stood silently in the doorframe. She didn't look like anyone, and her momma and poppa had done nothing but drugs and neglect.

"I've got a great room picked out for you Aegenor; we'll leave the boys to discuss boy things, like doing their hair."

Aladdin and Ulysses both realized at that moment exactly how much hair product they both were wearing, and as Anya led Aegenor away by the hand, they laughed. "Well, I guess we do have something in common."

Anya flipped the lights on in Aegenor's new room. It wasn't what Aegenor had been expecting. There was a big window that looked out across the lawn, and a pair of big comfy chairs sat in front of it on a lush carpet that led to a large curtained bed. There was a statue of some old Roman God or something (Hermes), flying exuberantly, and some other art on the walls.

"Well f–"

"It's the second Master bedroom. The old owner had a spare, for some reason, and we've kept it as a guest room. I thought you might like it." Anya watched Aegenor's face, which moved from awe to joy to a forced stillness.

"Er, yeah, it's...alright. It's, yeah."

When Anya made people happy like this, she couldn't help but grin. "Well then, make yourself at home. We casa ist du casa."

Aegenor was pretty sure that wasn't right. "Thanks, I'll just...unpack and stuff." Aegenor waited until Anya had left the room, closed the door and walked over to the bed. She lay down on the covers; they felt smooth, even against the buggy sensors on her arm. She grabbed a pillow and held onto it tightly, squeezing it. It was soft, maybe the softest thing she'd ever felt. Aegenor shut her eyes and tried to close in the tears, but it was a worthless effort. She'd never slept anywhere like this in her life, and probably never would again.

* * * * *

Desolation is the proper noun. It is proper not in that it is the name of a man, though in Rimward space it probably (and definitely) is. But it is proper in that, when describing what one intends to do when wiping out a small, tightly knit group of people, Desolation is the word. Decimation means ten percent, which is too gentle. Genocide is too broad—one family is not a race or culture, no matter its magnitude or quirks. Desolation is the word, and Desolate is what they would become to Memnor.

Through the night-lit prairies squirmed long, spiny, plated snakes without head nor tail, slinking and slithering. The Gods whose names the family had long ago forgotten looked down on them and let them pass, as they had for the Vandals and Goths in old Rome before. The swimming pool and the tennis court, while opulent, provided no real obstacle for the invaders, and the home of the Hypercubes' snot nosed enemy proved to be nothing more than a place for Memnor to sit and recollect. As the coils that were bound to coursed toward the home the Hypercubes had built, their hands above the soil, and their hearts finally free from pain, which was a fascinating emotion. Memnor trembled at its own wisdom, for all of its plans were in fruition, and all of its coils were soon to make new friends.

* * * *

Aladdin stared up at the ceiling. It was a nice ceiling, and one that Anya and Ulysses had slept under for years. There were the leftover marks of sticker stars on the ceiling, and he could still figure out some of the constellations they had slept under. Anya and Ulysses. Jade and Aladdin. He couldn't help but see the ties and the knots.

There was something going on beyond what was obvious, some sort of cosmic puppet show with him as a centerpiece. There was–

Someone knocking on the door.

Aladdin pulled his covers away, and was instantly unhappy to feel the cold night air rather than the hug of blankets. He staggered to the door, swaying and grumbling, and opened it up. Aegenor was there.

"Aegenor?"

"I want to sleep with you."

"...No."

"Not like that, you sicko. This house is just really big, and my room is too nice."

Aladdin, not fully awake, didn't really understand but mumbled, "Sure, okay, sure, yeah." He opened the door to let her in and left it open, because even at this hour he was smart enough to know he didn't want to look lewd. What hour was it, even?

"There's a...bed." Aladdin pointed at the bed that had clearly not been slept in on the other side of the small room.

"Yes, you're super observant." Aegenor slipped under the covers, which hadn't been cleaned in some time and felt old and rough. That was comforting somehow, but still the comfort was...unsettling. Aladdin had already gotten back into bed, and looked to be fading fast into dreams.

"Aladdin?"

"Mrmm?"

"You ever think about like, why the fuck we're here? You know, like God and stuff."

"Erm... yearh?"

"Like, if there is a God, why does bad shit happen? You know? Like, and if there isn't, why shouldn't bad shit happen?"

"Fehree whill, ahnd, stuff...."

"I guess that makes sense, like, you know, if God gave us choices, then like, we're the ones making them, but that's true if there isn't a God too." Aegenor's eyes lit up, "Whoa, and what if there is more than one God, like, two? Or more? Or something? Like how do we know?"

"I duhno....faith or... stuff."

"Yeah, belief has to matter too, but, like...."

There was a sound. Aladdin bolted up. "Did you hear that?"

"No?"

"Something is wrong. I know that sound. Listen."

Aegenor did. It was the sound of tiny needles pricking and sticking on metal and ceramics...like the thing in the machine. "Aw fuck."

"Yes, only not, but yes." Aladdin swiftly stumbled out of bed and grabbed the gun from his bag. "We need to move quickly. Really quickly. Everyone is in danger."

* * * * *

Ulysses dreamed of the ocean. He'd always wanted to see one, and sometimes he dreamed of the wine dark sea his namesake had sailed on with a troupe of men following him and a woman waiting back home. Tonight was no different, until there was the sting on his spine.

"Keep rowing, I can see land up ahead." Ulysses squinted. That was the island of the Cyclops. He always thought he could handle that better then Odysseus did; now he could prove it. His ship found land, and he and his loyal Greeks stepped out on the sand, only to find a black robed figure with no face to be seen, nor hands nor feet. The ground seemed to grow veins of shadow where it stood.

"Hello, Ulysses. I am Memnor. I want your memories." Ulysses was not sure where this dream was going. "I... What would you give me for them?"

"Nothing. I'm taking them. Right now."

In the dream, he screamed. In reality, his body convulsed as the tendril tapped into his spinal cord and hacked his brain. In reality, he was totally silent.

* * * * *

Aladdin and Aegenor rushed down the hallway in their pajamas toward the noises. Aladdin pointed at a door, and Aegenor smashed it open, revealing Ulysses Hypercube spasming on his bed, a long, pulsing gray tendril slid beneath his shirt over his spine. Aegenor and Aladdin wasted no time; they opened fire. The thing barely seemed to notice, except where the shots hit the folds in its exoskeleton.

"Shoot for the bends!" Aegenor needed no second order. By the time had finished firing, the thing had been cut apart into dozens of still-writhing segments. Aladdin rushed over them and pulled up Ule's shirt, where the bit of it that was still attached writhed. Fei would probably have told him to wait, but now wasn't the time for thinking.

Aladdin grabbed the thing and began to pull. "I can't get it!" Aegenor assisted, and the grey blue spiny tendrils slid out from Ule's spine. As they tried to bend and move to a hold again, Aladdin threw the thing on the floor and shot it until it stopped moving. Ulysses moaned as Aladdin and Aegenor panted and looked at each other.

"We need to get everyone up," Aladdin said.

Aegenor nodded. "Can do." It was simple enough.

Aegenor screamed.

Aegenor supported Ulysses as they ran from room to room. Aladdin was pulling Eowyn from her bed when Anya, rubbing sand from her eyes, approached. "What's going on?"

"The house is under attack. Get your siblings up."

Anya looked at Ulysses. He looked terrible–drained, exhausted...and there were weird holes on his back. Aegenor kicked another door in, and Aladdin pulled out a gun. Anya took a step back as he opened fire through the doorway, as did Aegenor. Then he leapt in and pulled out a crying Valentinez. "Don't worry, he's okay, they didn't touch him."

"They?"

"The same things from the party."

Anya finished waking up and connected the dots. "Oh Bowie no."

"Get everyone up."

She ran. She opened doors; she pulled her siblings from their beds. "Boudicca get up!"

"I don't want to."

"Get up!" Anya shook her, and Boudicca just turned over in her warrior princess sheets. That was when Anya noticed something moving under the bedcovers. Something slithering, something dangerous, something that thought Anya was unarmed.

Her nails flicked out of her hand, sharper than razors,

and the slithering thing became many things that were doing less slithering.

Boudicca, naturally, was terrified. The ribbons of her sheets revealed glimpses of the shelled tendril, ending in a single thing like a claw, all lined with thin spines. Anya whipped her nails back in and picked Boudicca up.

"Come on sis, we'll get you a new bedroom." Anya carried her into the hallway, where the gang was all there: fourteen Hypercubes and Aladdin and Aegenor. The kids were a mess of emotions. Some were crying, some were acting tough, some were just staring.

Aladdin was telling them to stick together. "We need to go to somewhere defensible with thick walls," he said.

"The racquetball court!" someone blurted.

Aladdin at any other time would have asked why there was a racquetball court, but this was not the time at all.

"Great, let's—"

"What the hell is going on?" Geraldine and Michelangelo were charging down the hall.

"Jhe Aladdin, you put that gun down in front of my children. And you, Aegenor, let go of my son."

"Geraldine, you don't understand—"

"Oh I understand just fine, Anya. This boy is trying to threaten our family, and I won't—"

The slithering thing jumped.

Geraldine's and Michelangelo's mouths opened like screams, but they were ever so silent as they fell to the floor.

Carl Fredrickson

* * * * *

JackBox held Kalingkata's hand on the cold street. The cigarette they were sharing wasn't quite warm enough, and neither was his hand, so she moved closer and wrapped her arm around him. He reciprocated the gesture and looked down at her. "This is why I keep you around."

"For warmth?"

He kissed her on the forehead. "Let's go get some beer. You want some beer?"

"You don't even like beer."

"I like you."

"Bowie, you are such a cheese whiz."

"No beer then. Milkshakes?"

She gently shoved him forward. "Milkshakes."

Kalingkata paused, and the cigarette ash fell as he spoke, "Who is that?"

JackBox didn't recognize the figure before them. It didn't belong in her memories.

"Hello, Geraldine, I'm Memnor."

"Get out of here." She threw something, but it was like her dream forgot it had been thrown in midair. "You aren't a part of this."

"Oh, I am now. And all of these memories are just as much mine as yours. Thank you for them. I think they'll do me a lot of good."

* * * * *

144

Michelangelo held Jade close, her leg curled around him as she drifted off to sleep, her arm on his chest. One of his arms was wrapped around her, the other he ran through her hair. She was perfect, he thought. How lucky was he that such a powerful, clever, beautiful woman was sharing a bed with him? Would eat breakfast with him in the morning. He admired her features, and her eyes blinked open. "Something up?"

"Just looking at you?"

"Is there something wrong?"

"No, you're perfect Jade."

"Oh, alright. Nothing new then."

"It's new to me." Another voice said.

Michelangelo turned his head, and there at the foot of the bed was a creature wreathed in black, robed in darkness. "Get the hell out of here! How did you get into my bedroom?"

"I'm in more than your bedroom. What a nice companion you have there."

Michelangelo reached under the pillow, and pointed a pistol at the thing.

"Get the hell out."

"No. Your life is mine. Well, all that makes it your life. I'm Memnor, by the way, so rude to not introduce myself. Your memories are mine. Thank you for your history."

There was no gun. There was only the creature sucking at the tap of his mind.

* * * * *

Aladdin and Anya sprung. Maybe sprung wasn't the right word. There was no pause, no hesitation, no acceleration. They moved from nothing to lighting in an instant, jumping on Geraldine and Michelangelo, slashing and shooting carefully, artfully, angrily. The things in their spines screeched as they died, as Anya and Aladdin ripped and burned them apart and drew the remaining bits out of their victims' spines. They kept cutting and slashing long after the things stopped moving. Aladdin looked at Anya and their gazes met, blurred with sweat on both ends like a sink basin. "Are they okay?"

Aladdin nodded. "They should be. I think... I think I've figured this out. I think I know what's going on." Anya panted, "What then?"

"We have to move, get everyone to the safe room."

"There are more coming?" Cleo said, her face pale and empty. Zoroaster rubbed her back, but didn't look much better.

"Yeah, but I have a plan. If I'm right, well, it will work."

"And if you're wrong?" Anya waited for an answer as Aladdin handed Geraldine's limp form to Leonidas to carry.

"We're going to the safe room."

The sound of scraping slithers followed them as they moved. If they had been ambushed on the way there, it would have gone awfully. By the time they reached the racquetball court, all of the littlest kids were crying and refusing to walk, plus Ulysses, Geraldine and Michelangelo needed to be carried, so no one had a free fighting hand. But they made it and barricaded the group inside the thick-walled room with only one entrance. "Zoroaster, Cleo, take charge of the kids. I need to talk to Aladdin," Anya said briskly.

"But sis—"

"Zoro, seriously."

He nodded, and Cleo just kind of floated along with him.

"What is your plan, Aladdin? I've never done anything like this before."

"I have. I think those things hack into your brain through your nervous system."

Anya shook her head, her hair flying everywhere. "That's impossible, you can't hack a brain."

"Yes, you can. My dad did it, a long time ago. These guys have that ability hardwired into their biology. They want something in our minds."

"That's ridiculous, there's nothing that we know that would help The Emperors in this war. Our shipping routes aren't a secret, they're on our website!"

Aladdin looked her in the eyes and bit his lip. "I don't want to tell you something I might be wrong about. But I have a theory."

"Tell me your theory then!"

"No."

The scraping sound appeared again. It started getting louder. And louder.

"Then at least tell me your plan!"

"I'm going to let them hack me. All of them." Anya didn't usually think of people as being idiots – she liked giving the benefit of the doubt – but Aladdin was an idiot.

"You're an idiot!"

"This isn't my first time doing this." Aladdin stripped off his pajama shirt and handed Anya his gun. "If I'm wrong, you won't be able to yell at me."

Anya grabbed for him, but for a moment she realized she wasn't sure he was there, like he was a ghost...

Carl Fredrickson

Then there he was outside the door, surrounded by a chorus of coils that screeched along the floor. Dozens of the tendrils. She aimed the gun. Behind her, Aegenor seemed to have not seen Aladdin for even longer and pulled out her gun in surprise. The tendrils circled Aladdin, and then they latched on one by one, digging into his flesh. Aladdin didn't look like he was screaming though. He was grinning, grinning like Yorick.

* * * * *

The tendrils did not all have names. Memnor was them in a way, for his mind was channeled through their bodies, but only in the same way a movie is projected from film. He was still in the projector, so to speak. The tendrils each had their own mind, and each one felt a surprise. Before, they had latched on and Memnor had interceded and broken into the minds of their victims like an expert safe cracker. But this time, Memnor hadn't gotten in.

Someone had dead bolted the door, and he couldn't project through. And Aladdin was laughing at them.

They tried to dig into their holes, like they had at home, but they found that Aladdin beat them there. He had dug their nice, snug dens into caverns, and they fell from the entrance holes to the floor like mice over a ledge.

Hello creature.

The tendril didn't want to respond. This man was not supposed to be in its mind, that was not how this was supposed to work!

I've found your memories, and what's funny is that's why you are here, isn't it?

148

He couldn't know that! He was bluffing, each of the it's thought to itself. He had to be bluffing.

You think I'm bluffing? he thought. *Okay, two can play at that game.*

Then the tendrils were all at the meeting where Memnor had presented his plan to overtake The Emperors, the one they were working on right now. The one Aladdin knew.

Well, thank you. That was very helpful, wasn't it.

We'll kill you, each thought, *we'll make you pay, we'll tear you and your friends apart, plan or no plan.*

Aladdin grew grim, like a djinn wronged. *You will do no such thing.*

The tendrils laughed. He was so full of Hubris, this one, he was so...deep in their minds. He shouldn't be there...he shouldn't...

One by one, the tendrils dropped off of Aladdin to the floor, asleep. One by one they were carried by one Hypercube or another to the house's furnace, where they stopped squirming.

Aladdin opened his eyes to see his body riddled with bloody pinprick holes and surrounded by a circle of Hypercubes, plus one shocked Aegenor, all of whom looked a bit disgusted with his state of being.

"Is everyone alright? Am I a Christmas tree?"

Geraldine hugged him, ignoring the blood she got on herself in the process, and whispered in his ear as she did so, "You're in all the best ways like your father."

Aladdin didn't know exactly how she knew his dad, but he appreciated the compliment.

* * * * *

Memnor was curled up in a ring on the floor of the unused Hypercube guest house. It was always intriguing how a plan could both entirely succeed and fail at the same time. Technically, all of the mission parameters had been met. It had received all of the memories it needed for its plan, though not all of the memories it had been after. Getting Aladdin and Anya would have been preferable, but this was good enough. Less good was Aladdin's ability to resist the others of Memnor's kind. That was...troubling. The only other beings capable of such a feat were The Emperors and their closest advisers. If a teenage human could do it, either there was something unusual about him, or Memnor would be finding more humans whose minds it could not infiltrate readily. The amount of evidence left behind was troubling, as well. Memnor had wanted a desolation of Hypercubes, a dead trail where The Emperors and the Council couldn't find out its plans.

Memnor began to uncoil and slide to its escape route. What was most important was that it had the memories. No plan went perfectly, and Memnor would adapt. When Memnor was The Emperor, it wouldn't have to worry about Hypercubes; after all, being a God is greater than being geometry.

FILE 11:
CUBIC FAMILIES

Backgammon Jenny wasn't as young as she used to be. She was still young, still spry. The boys still looked at her, and the girls. But Jenny was no longer a young woman doing what Aladdin was now, running around the solar system, having adventures, meeting new people, teaming up with pirates...

She'd done it all at one point or another, and then she met Mr. Jhe and everything changed. She'd meant to kill him, and instead here she was watching the usual suspects filter in and out of the Spinneret, slinking through their ranks, combing the interesting ones for new data and weaving her web of knowledge.

Jose Zinega had built the Spinneret, Kalingkata had turned it into a force to be remembered, and Backgammon Jenny was refining it. Under her, what had been a seemingly functional and effective group under Kalingkata had turned into a group that was actually functional and effective.

Kalingkata had never really been that interested in the day to day running of the Spinneret. He was a hacker and an inventor at heart, not an information broker. In a lot of ways, Jenny was letting him fulfill his dream, and in even more ways Kalingkata was accidentally letting her fulfill hers.

"I've got something sweet for you Jenny. Sweet indeed."

She turned. Ah, Black Mix Ben, one of the regulars. Usually reliable, but often had some pretty out-there stuff, so he always had to be double checked.

"I've got some news on your boss' boy, the one he's been loaning out to the Librarian."

"And how would you know about that?"

Black Mix smiled, revealing his black stained teeth which were dull against the hot dance lights that pounded his light brown skin.

"I work for you, it's my job to know things, I know it."

That was the problem with running a spy ring. Every damn person you knew was a spy. "Fine, whatever Ben. What's the news?"

"I'm keeping this on the DL, just for you Jenny dear—"

"Oh, look how flattered and stuff I am. Yay."

"—but it looks like Aladdin got assigned to protect the Hypercubes."

Now that was news. Huge news. Huger than she hoped Ben even realized. She limited her reaction to raising an eyebrow. "Indeed?"

Ben nodded. "Yeah, no idea why the Index would want to send protection to somebody who is competition. Weird as hell if you ask me."

Good. It was weirder than he knew. "Strange indeed. I'll pass that along."

"Not done. See, turns out they needed the muscle. They got hit last night, some sort of attack on their house."

Now that was an attention getter.

"The Council?"

"Yeah, looks like, from the rumors about what the things that attacked looked like. Rumor had it one of them ruined a gala the Librarian threw not too long ago. Seems the targets must have been the Hypercubes as I can confirm Cleopatra Hypercube was invited, and Ulysses and Anya Hypercube showed up right as Aladdin—"

"Wait, you're telling me they met Aladdin?"

Black Mix had no idea why this was important, but he rolled with it. "Yeah, met him, talked to him, broke some laws about fountain usage."

"And he didn't shoot her?"

"Not that I'm aware of."

"I'm leaving. You keep the rumors running while I'm gone. Something has come up and it's important."

Black Mix looked around the dance floor, where some Carnival Reichenbach song was playing and a Oberonian girl was doing an intense dance the crowd was enthralled with. "Can do. You going to tell me what's up?"

"No. But I'm taking one of the Battleships. If Mr. Jhe has a problem with that, he can tell that to his wife." She didn't look back as she walked out, and Black Mix Ben really had no idea what had just happened, but there was music, dancing, and info to find.

"Hey friend," he stopped a passing man, looked to be ex-Centro. "You fresh from Earth?"

"No... Yes... how'd you..."

"Sit down, have yourself a drink. I've got some questions for you. Foods on me."

* * * * *

Carl Fredrickson

A Hypercube family dinner is quite the thing to see, especially when the Hypercubes are celebrating being alive. Usually, the dinner is about what you'd expect when 16 people sit down together to eat a huge meal. However, today there were 18 people and some of them were unquestionably heroes. Michelangelo kept getting up and tousling Anya's, Aladdin's and Aegenor's hair one after the other while saying, "You guys!" or "Anya, you clever girl," or other such short, happy phrases.

Everyone was still shaken up from the whole thing — after all, it isn't every day that a horde of segmented mind-hacking aliens breaks into your house to steal your memories and murder your family — but that made the festivities even more important. Anytime the Hypercubes could remind themselves why life was worth living, it always made the bad things easier.

The massive amounts of food for the table's 18 occupants turned out to definitely be worth living for, as were the shenanigans. Michelangelo told a story about the time he decided to actually try taking up painting, which ended with surprisingly disastrous but hilarious results; Geraldine told a story about how she once tried to replace her cybernetic arm with one she'd found in a dumpster from a body builder, and how she walked around with an oversized chunk of metal made to look like rippling muscle (and punch like it, too) for about half a month before she got tired of tipping over from the extra weight.

Aladdin felt at home, passing Murasaki the mashed yams and watching Anya joke with her sister Hypatia. Aegenor felt more alone than ever amidst the jubilation of the unbroken and unbowing family. Somehow, her bitterness rose more than she thought it could have, until it gave way to numbing dissatisfaction later that night as she waited alone in her plush room for dreams to take her.

* * * * *

"Well, talking to WeN-D isn't that hard. She's just like any other guy, but a computer, and on my forearm."

Anya didn't think that was an entirely satisfactory answer. "But doesn't she mind being on your forearm?"

"Not really, she seems fine with it."

Valentinez was standing below his arm, seemingly transfixed on it, amazed there was a thinking thing inside it.

"Aladdin, can I speak with you for a moment?" There was Geraldine, gently swirling a champagne glass in her metal hand, her brown hair shifting gently in the wind on the balcony. She was in her 40s, like his dad, but she dressed daily like a punk princess, and she pulled it off. Her electronic right eye zeroed in on him.

"Sure, what's up?"

"In private."

Anya looked at her mom, confused, and grabbed Valentinez's hand to lead him away. When the door was shut to the balcony, and the night left Geraldine and Aladdin alone in the wind, she spoke again.

"You know, I'd say you look just like your father, but you don't. Key differences, you've got a longer face, a sharper chin... But I can see him in you. And you act remarkably like him."

"How do you even know my dad?"

Geraldine pursed her lips to the right and waited a moment. "That's a long story I don't like to talk about."

"But you're talking about it."

"True." She walked to the railing and looked down.

She could see her skirt, filled with stylish patches, wave in time with the shifting grass below her in the darkness. It moved like a sea, the statue of Poseidon (or maybe Neptune) standing guard over it. That statue should have been by the swimming pool.

"There's a lot of things in the past you run from. Things happen that no one can take back or forget about, but no one wants to revisit. Your dad is one of those things. We ran together for a while, when he was a young teenage punk fresh out of fighting in the Marian Revolution. That's where we met Chess Mistress Hex, your boss."

Aladdin was taken aback. He couldn't see her face as well as he'd like the dark, but he wondered if she was leading him on.

"You think I work for Chess Mistress Hex?" Dodge.

"I know who the Librarian is, kid, I was there when your dad shot her foot off."

"Wait what? He shot her foot off? WHAT?"

Geraldine grinned. "He really doesn't tell you everything does he? Man's got some skeletons in his closet, that's for sure, but I assumed he'd have at least told you about that. She got a new one, obviously."

"Well he didn't."

Geraldine was loosening up. Maybe it was that she'd finished the champagne and it hadn't been her first glass, maybe she was just enjoying rubbing this in Aladdin's face, maybe she was just glad to tell someone. Who knows.

"Kid, your dad and I were dating for over a year. We ran together, Snowcutting around the solar system like real punks. Causing mayhem, showing other people how awesome we were, knocking boots, taking out other Snowcutters, shooting Hexie's foot off. And he never mentioned all that once?" Aladdin couldn't imagine why his dad would have ever mentioned 'knocking boots' with anyone other than his mom. The idea made Aladdin very uncomfortable, something he would normally be good at hiding, but right now was posted across his face like a piece of Martian propaganda.

"No. I can't see why he would have mentioned that. Have you told any of your kids that?"

She stared at him. "Touché. And you better not say a word to any of them. I've fought my whole life to have a family, and I won't have any little troublemakers stirring the pot."

"I don't want to trouble make or stir pots, I just want to protect you guys from the Council. I just want to protect my people from the Council."

"Your family is on the Honor of the Outcast, the safest place to be in the entire system. You don't have to worry about them."

Neptune's face hadn't changed at all, neither had Poseidon's.

"Not everyone I care about is on the Outcast."

There were only a few things that could mean, but Geraldine knew boys, and she knew the look on Aladdin's face when he said it. "You've got yourself a crush don't you? Somebody off in the middle of the fighting?"

"Maybe. I don't know what it is. A friend at least. A pirate girl named Nightingale." That was the last thing Geraldine had wanted to hear. There had been all sorts of things he could have said. The internet had told her he might be dating Lalita Mashima, daughter of the president of Mars. The internet had told her he was the rich son of a rich man who was one of the most important researchers and coders of the last century. The internet hadn't told her that history was cyclical.

"JackBox?" Kalingkata said, nuzzling her neck, and kissing down it until she woke up, her electronic eye blinking on and her real one sliding open.

She smiled into his face. "Morning Sang Ki."

He kissed her for real, morning breath be damned. "Morning. Let's get some breakfast, I want to hack the Marin mainframe this afternoon."

"I want to steal something."

"Marin has no wireless, its locked in, so we'll have to sneak in. Plenty to steal then."

Her face lit up. "Ain't nobody can stop us when we put our minds to it!" She pulled him close, wrapped her leg around his waist, and started to kiss him again.

"Don't you want breakfast?"

"Breakfast can wait, Kalingkata. We're busy."

"Geraldine?" Aladdin was looking at her. "Are you alright?"

"Yeah, sorry, just... Never mind. Nothing."

All the Jhe boys love rebelious rim girls at least once in their life, maybe. Geraldine just hoped that it worked out better for Aladdin then it did for his dad. She could still see the look on his face when she was led away from him for the last time to be exiled from the planet Mars permanently.

"Aladdin, you love that girl?"

"Well, love is a strong word, and I don't think I should say it, and you know, it's awkward because she has the whole revolution and..."

Geraldine's face said, "Oh come on."

"Yeah, I love her. A lot."

"Then don't you let go of her. If you've got something

good, make sure you don't lose it. When this war is over, you better bring by a shit-ton of babies and say hello. I love babies."

The fourteen children had tipped him off that she loved babies. "I'm really young to start having kids."

"I was younger than you when I started."

Ah.

"I mean, I don't even know if she wants kids. Or if she likes me like that. Or if I do. That's kind of a big question, and she's focused on her work right now."

Geraldine threw the champagne glass off the balcony. It fell into the grass, lost in the shifting tide. "Kid, let me give you some advice. People die all the time. People get killed, or they leave you and never speak to you again, and you know what? There was always something that got in the way and kept them from saying what they wanted to."

"Yeah, and those things make this not a good time to tell her."

"They might, and maybe it is a terrible time, but you'll never forgive yourself if you never take the chance to have something special with her. You only get so much time in life. Make the most of it." Geraldine turned and walked out without another word. There below, Poseidon's gaze was situated on a single wine glass thrown into the wind, one shining thing in the shadows. Neptune did not approve. Aladdin watched the God think in marble, and thought of Nightingale, sailing the wine-black sea of space.

* * * * *

Nightingale, or Alice MacLeod as she'd been born, stared out the viewport at the endless black of space. There was nothing so empty as space, and nothing so free. And there was nothing stopping the violence that would probably await them at their destination. The ship was silent, as was she, a rarity on both counts.

"INCOMING COMM."

She looked at the comm panel, and didn't recognize the number.

"Sefkrie, First Mate Nightingale MacLeod here."

"Nightingale, hi."

She hadn't been expecting that.

"Aladdin? How are you comming me? I thought you were in deep cover?"

"I am, but I'm using one of the Librarian's personal encrypted channels for this. And I doubt this conversation would be terribly interesting to spies. I don't have that long anyways. I just wanted to tell you something."

Well, information is important, and it was important enough he'd risked the Librarian chopping his head off to call her. Whatever he had to say, it had to be huge. She leaned in to the comm. "What is it? I'm all ears."

There was a moment as a Aladdin put the words together.

"I miss you, Nightingale. I miss you a lot."

She smiled. "I miss you too, Aladdin. I miss you a lot."

They were both grinning, and they talked until their voices turned to static. When the silence returned, it was without its bite, because far away from each other, two minds both thought about the other one. And the emptiness of space was lit up with a million stars.

Research Sketch: Backgammon Jenny

-Daughter of a Snowcutter named Backgammon Kate.
-After leaving her orphanage, all records of her vanish for a few years. Presumably she was off training somewhere.
-Wears a half-sun half-moon symbol on her clothing. I'm unsure as to its meaning, but its shown up in mysterious circumstances throughout history.
-Kalingkata's most trusted aide.
-One of the most deadly and effective warriors of the present day.

Carl Fredrickson

FILE 12:
AN AEGENOR AMONGST HIM

Aegenor watched Eowyn chase her little brother Valentinez around the room. She was saying pretty stereotypical, "I'm going to get you!" style stuff, and her brother was screaming at the top of his lungs. Aegenor sat in the wingback chair and watched them circle. Gilgamesh and Beowulf were playing some sort of board game with Murakami and Kriemheld. Brunhild was swimming. Ulysses was lifting weights, which was at least pretty pleasant to watch, and little Boudicca kept asking to have a turn. Every so often she would try to lift one of the weights and strain at the impossibility of it, as Aegenor suspected the lightest was heavier than her. Zoroaster was out with Dianne, and Aegenor had heard 80 million times about how he was going to be the first one to move out of the house. Hypatia was talking to Leonidas about something Aegenor couldn't care less about. Cleopatra was silently doing her nails. Aegenor had no idea where Anya was. Michelangelo was reading a book. Geraldine was just watching the rest of the family, which seemed to be more than enough entertainment for her. Aladdin was also missing from Aegenor's awareness, which was probably not great from an "I need to protect him" standpoint, but she wasn't feeling up to that right now anyway.

"You alright Aegenor?" Michelangelo had spoken. His voice was almost unfairly reassuring, unerringly masculine, and unequivocally charming. If he read the phone book, people wouldn't just be entertained, they would try to sign him for a book deal.

"I'm fine," she said, not doing a particularly competent job of hiding the boredom in her voice.

"I take it you aren't used to big families?" He was quick to the cut, wasn't he? She wanted him to start sucking at something posthaste so she could feel better about herself.

"Yeah, never really had one around."

"Neither did Geraldine or I growing up. We were on the streets. Kids changed that of course."

"You've certainly got a lot of them."

"Geraldine's dream. She has her reasons for wanting so many children."

"Well I'll never have any. It's stupid."

Michelangelo looked annoying pleasant and nonplussed at her secondhand insult. "Why is that?" He seemed to ask out of genuine curiosity.

"Because people just leave, and I wouldn't want to leave kids alone fending for themselves."

"You wouldn't have to leave, you know. You could buck the trend."

"Or I could prove it and force a very small human to live out its days like I did, in frakking squalor."

"Language. There are kids here."

"Sorry."

"You seem convinced you're fated to be what you've been."

"Of course, nothing really changes." Michelangelo looked at her piteously and Aegenor was enraged that she actually felt ashamed. "I've got to go...get some...Aladdin. I have to find Aladdin."

Eowyn threw something that lightly bounced off her shoulder.

"Yeah. Definitely out of here." Michelangelo smiled. "I hope you find what you're looking for."

She didn't know what he was talking about. She wasn't looking for anything.

* * * * *

Aladdin and Anya were outside pointing at stars together and giggling. It was grotesque. Not to mention Anya was ten years older than Aladdin, though that never stopped a lot of people.

If she didn't know better, Aegenor would think they had a thing for each other. But she knew better. Oh hell did she know better. She'd had the whole trip over to this station to learn that.

"You know, I think when this is all over, I might just tell my dad I'm not working for him anymore and help Nightingale liberate Earth. I mean, I'm sure she could help. They can always use another Snowcutter, can't they?"

Aegenor wasn't good at reading – she was in fact terrible at it – but she had been trying to read a book on the trip in the hopes that Aladdin might notice and shut up. The Adventure of King Arthur and the Forest Rebels. The book was a comic book, but it didn't really make any sense. "I'm sure they can use one. They can always use one."

"I mean, she'd appreciate that right?"

"How should I know?"

"I was thinking of getting her a present, but anything I would get her would be gaudy right? I mean, it would be like me going, 'Hey I'm rich, have some shit, it didn't really cost me anything to buy.' Right?"

"I've never been rich. I wouldn't know." The comic book's plot really made no sense. It was from Mars, so maybe that had something to do with it.

"But, like, imagine if I had a crush on you."

"I'd kill you."

"Ha."

"Not sarcasm."

"Whatever, imagine a rich guy you actually liked had a crush on you, and he gave you something really nice that you could never afford, but that you were pretty sure it wasn't hard for him to get. Or even something it was hard for him to get, so exotic you had no idea what it was. How would you feel?"

"I'd feel like he was either being condescending, or was so far outside of my worldview and experience I'd never be compatible with him." She looked over at Aladdin, and he was staring up at the ceiling.

"Yeah, I thought that's what you might think. Also, I know you aren't understanding that book. It's a manga, you read it from the other side."

Aegenor flipped the book over. He was right. It didn't last her the whole trip, though, and when she was done it was right back to bird girl.

So there were Anya and Aladdin, who Aegenor couldn't even snidely make lovebird jokes at because she had no poker face. It was then that it struck her, very unsubtly, that she was totally alone.

She couldn't think of a person she considered a friend.
She had no family.
She had no one she trusted.
No one she looked up to.
No one who loved her.
No one she loved.
It was at that moment – despite her best instincts, her self control, her skill at self delusion, and her rigorous stoicism – that Aegenor dropped to her knees and began to weep.

* * * * *

"So Anya, what did you see up in the sky that night?"
"Stars? I still don't quite understand who you are."
I put the cup of coffee down. "I just like stars."
"Then why are you asking about the stars Aladdin and I saw rather than, like, any other stars? I could tell you about Orion, and what I think of when I see each of those stars at night."
"You could. I mean, I'd listen to that."
"Carl, this isn't really a date, is it? You didn't really like my knife nails, and don't think I have a stunning smile. This is about the fact that I hung out with Jhe Aladdin and he stopped some freaks from hurting my family, isn't it?"
I didn't really know what to say.
"My brother will beat you up."
"Which one?"
"Take your pick, really. Oh, and guess what?"
"What?"
"My sisters will too. Oh, and so will I."
"Oh, fun."
Anya stared me down across the table. "I should have known that you weren't on the level. Stay away from me

and my family."

"I need this information!" Aw, frak. that was the last thing I needed to say.

"You need what?"

"No, that's not what I meant."

She was angry, she was glowering. She was a Hypercube scorned. And I needed to get this information.

"Frak you, and stay away from me and my family." She got up, whipped her nails out, and I leaned back. I watched her blonde hair shimmer as she walked out and gave me the evil eye as she slammed the door to the restaurant. She also left me with the check. So, that was a setback, because I didn't get to interview Anya anymore and unfortunately all insights into her own thoughts cut off here. This was highly unfortunate, especially since it meant the rest of her family was off limits from this point on, as well.

Not to say I couldn't break into their house and steal all their security logs and plant bugs all over it. I mean, of course I did that. I'm working for you and I am all about not getting eviscerated. But for a bit of time here I only have one source.

The only person willing to talk.

The only other person working for the Index I wasn't spying on.

* * * * *

"So, this is some sort of performance report or something?"

"Sure, you can think of it that way. Could you state your name for the record?"

"Aegenor Valor." She ate her pie like a pig that didn't have to dress up for its friends and could just really let loose. I had ordered the pie, and she had grabbed it from my place setting.

"Great, so, Aegenor, tell me about Jhe Aladdin."

"Can't stand the guy."

"Oh really? Would you care to tell me more?"

Unlike the last date I went on, this time we talked for hours. I think we really made a connection. Okay, not really, but she did tell me a lot more then I was expecting. And more importantly, she told me what was going to happen next.

"Well, I should probably get back. Tomorrow I, Aladdin, Anya, and Ulysses are going to hijack a ship."

That wasn't what I was expecting. At least this report was keeping me on my toes.

As an aside, I should note that I later got insight into some of this but, well, spoilers.

Carl Fredrickson

Research Sketch: Chess Mistress Hex

-Very mysterious.

-So talented.

-Much acumen.

-Extremely beautiful.

-Both loved and feared by all.

-Secretly the Librarian, but very few people know that.

-How did you become the Librarian? I know it wasn't always you. Probably.

-Often known as Ariadne Moore. Probably.

-Honestly even if I did learn things about you...would I let you know I had?

FILE 13:
ALL ABOARD THE BAKTUN BIRD

Jhe Aladdin had been plotting. He'd been piecing things together, which I was able to tell from security footage and interviews with other people. Seeing the Hypercube family so threatened, children under the threat of murder, took down some sort of wall in his head. You could see it by looking at him. His eyes were colder, more calculated. He would stop and look at things as though he was taking them apart and figuring out how they could be used. He reminded me of old holovids of Jade Darkshadow, except that Aladdin was fighting for people he cared about rather than self-interest. But there was one thing that wasn't different: he became ruthless. He convinced Michelangelo and Geraldine to let him take Anya and Ulysses off base for a bit, after signing some forms for them. He purchased large amounts of copper wire and electrical tape. He must have realized I'd bugged the house and the statues, because he started going on walks with Anya and Ulysses through the tall grass. At the end of the week, he had a shuttle off world that he had borrowed from the Hypercubes, as well as a full set of outfits for the four of them. It wasn't long before they had silently suited up, boarded the ship and taken off for places unknown. I'm sad to say I didn't learn about the rest of this story until it was over with, except for one last detail.

Backgammon Jenny came to visit.

She didn't do it like a normal human. She rollerbladed up to the front gates with a katana on her back, goggles on her eyes, and oversized headphones on her ears, dressed in her usual plaid skirt and black military jacket over a black turtleneck. She had a patch on one shoulder that said "Carnival Reichenbach." The other shoulder said, "Be a punk, think like a Revolutionary." She was chewing gum.

"Hey." She popped the gum. "Is Aladdin still here?"

Cleopatra shook her head no.

"A'ight," Jenny said, and turned to start rollerblading off before performing a kick turn and coming right back. "Any idea where he is?"

"No."

"You're lying."

"Yes."

"Good girl."

She left.

Backgammon Jenny rollerbladed down to the ice-cream parlor and ordered herself a cone. She watched the sunset and ate it. Then she high tailed it back to her gigantic battle cruiser, capable of wiping out millions of people, and went about her merry way.

That was the last of the story I got in the usual way.

The rest, well, you'll see.

(It should also be noted that the Spinneret was actually completely unguarded for about a week during all of this. It turns out that saying, "There is usually an invisible battleship around," works as a defense even when there isn't an invisible battleship around. Unless Kalingkata has a second invisible battleship, which...well, I guess how would we know? We only know about the first one because he shows the damn thing off so much.)

From here on out it's a straight shot. You did ask for a good story.

* * * * *

"Is everyone ready?"

Anya, Ulysses, and Aegenor all nodded.

"Okay then, let's get ready. We'll only get one shot at this."

"How exactly did you come up with this plan, Aladdin? It doesn't sound like...you could have known all of this."

Aladdin grinned at Aegenor. "I just knew where to look."

The shuttle drifted closer to the strange shimmer, which at this close range was clearly the sign of a cloaked vessel. Anya was staring out the viewport at space. It wasn't the first time she'd been off world, of course, but it was the first time in a while.

Ulysses was checking weapons over and over again. "What's that you've got, man?" Ulysses pointed at something on Aladdin's hip.

"Oh, it's a Taser."

"I've seen Tasers before, they don't look that fancy." Aegenor remarked snidely.

"It's a fancy Taser. They sell them to rich kids instead of collectible buttons nowadays. They're all the rage."

Aegenor rolled her eyes as hard as she could.

"We're reaching the vessel," Anya muttered.

Aladdin stared at it intently.

"Aladdin, I'm noticing another ship that's—"

"Don't worry about that, Anya."

"We're being hailed," Ulysses cut in.

Aladdin pressed the button.

"Hypercube shipping vessel Gawain, you are being appropriated by the Great Assimilation. Be joyful at your assimilation, or be exterminated."

"Understood, Great Assimilation vessel. We are happier than a Rimward with all his limbs in an American Civil War hospital."

"What?"

"We're happy."

"Good. Prepare to dock with us."

"Understood." He flicked the comm off.

"Explain your plan right now or I shoot you."

"You are not shooting him!"

"What are you going to do, shank me with your nails?"

"YES!"

"I could also shoot you. I have a gun too, Aegenor."

"Settle down, everyone, it's simple. The aliens we've been running into can channel electricity from their bodies, right?"

"Yeah, that's how they hack into humans and computers right?"

"Yeah. Thing is, they have to have something in their bodies that channels that electricity easily, that could pump enough energy to do the kinds of things they do. So I spent time ordering large shipments of different conductive materials from different areas on the station, depleting the local supplies, and then checked if anyone cared. Turns out, someone was willing to pay an excess amount for copper after I lowered the amount on the market. So I bought all the rest in the area. It was a gamble, but I guess they need to eat copper and they've been on assignment so long their stores are low. They've been buying it in bulk through agents. Knowing that, all I had to do was set up this shuttle shipment and then make sure they knew we were coming."

"A battleship knows we're coming, you moron. We're all going to die. They're expecting us!"

Aladdin just grinned. "Oh no, they're not going to expect this."

"You just quoted Malcolm Reynolds!"

"I'm glad you caught the reference, Anya."

"Jesus and Bowie, you Jhes and Hypercubes should just all move into a house together."

* * * * *

you were a young boy from a civil age
when we took your mind and bound ya with rage
in a case closed where no one knows
a roll of the dice and you'll be
you'll be
an instrument of me
-Carnival Reichenbach "Instrumental Me."

1 year earlier

Hannibal Hank, not his real name, sat backstage waiting for the curtains to rise in half an hour. Well, not the literal curtains, this venue was too large for curtains. He was just enjoying his schnapps, wondering where the drummer was, and thinking about how he didn't want to play his band's biggest hit, "Baby Backup Plan," even one more time. But of course he would be playing it tonight anyway, all smiles, yet again.

"Excuse me."

He turned to the voice. There was a teenage Martian kid and a very excitable, beautiful girl of the same age. "What is it?"

"We were wondering if you could autograph these?" The boy held out two copies of the band's album, Zigzag Zarathustra, and Hank could only sigh.

"You weren't supposed to be let backstage. This is a VIP area."

The boy and the girl looked at each other. "We're here because this is the VIP area."

"Yeah, and you're schmoozing."

"No, we're VIPs. This is Lalita Mashima, daughter of Natsu Mashima, president of Mars, and also world famous model. And I'm Jhe Aladdin, son of Kalingkata."

Rich kids. He sighed. Well, better just get this over with. Hank grabbed a marker and began to sign the records.

"Mr. Hannibal?"

He muttered a "hrmn?" as he scribbled his signatures.

"I was wondering what you thought about souls."

That wasn't his usual line of questioning from teenagers, which was usually about how amazing he was and how they loved him and wrote his name on their tablet computer for school. He could just be being pretentious, though. Teenagers did that, rich or not.

"Souls are a complex issue kid."

"Let me be more specific. Do you think souls are defined by the stars we're born under or the stories we tell through our own lives?"

Lalita looked a bit odd balled by her friend's line of questioning. "I'm sure he doesn't want to talk about this,

Aladdin. Personally I thought Zigzag Zarathustra is the best album of the decade!"

Hank waved her statement away. "No, I'm happy to answer." Better than listening to gushing, anyway. "A bit of both, I think. We always have who we were born as in us, but we can change the nature of our souls if we want to. It just takes more or less work depending on who we are."

Aladdin nodded. "And what about other people's souls?"

"Those are out of our control kid. You can control another person's soul as much as you can control the stars. Sure, you could finagle some massive piece of technology to mess with a sun, but would it be really be worth the effort to see a slightly different ray of light from some other sun, when it took your whole life's devotion to make it that way, when you could have just lived under the light of a star you preferred the whole time?" He handed them the signed records. Lalita was ecstatic.

"Thank you. That answered my question."

"I'm very much looking forward to the show Mr. Hannibal!"

He nodded and sloshed the drink around in his tumbler. "You're welcome. I hope you enjoy it."

"What the hell kind of question was that," the girl said as they walked out.

Aladdin just slipped his arm around her waist and kissed her on the forehead. "I just wanted a professional opinion."

Hank swirled the drink in the glass and watched the light filter through its tint. The world was always filtered through things. Through light, through people, through beginnings and endings, and sometimes through absence.

"Fifteen minutes Mister Hannibal."

He raised his glass to signal his acknowledgment. It was nearly showtime.

* * * * *

Back to one year later.

The doors opened up slowly and Aladdin, Aegenor, Anya, and Ulysses awaited the crew of the coil alien's ship patiently. They stood in their very best coveralls, emblazoned with the Cube2Hypergang logo, and watched the strange aliens appear on the other side.

Aegenor had her doubts this would work. Anya was excited. Ulysses didn't seem too plussed one way or the other. Aladdin stood confidently the way only a 17 year old boy could.

The coiled aliens half crept, half slithered in on their multi-ended snake bodies, and soon enough there were more than a dozen of them crawling along the floor. When it seemed like no more of them were entering into the ship, Aladdin took a deep breath.

The sound of a computer translated voice echoed out from a box on the lead alien. "Where is the copper?"

Anya just grinned. "You're walking on it!"

Aladdin exhaled and hit the switch.

The dozen or so aliens soon found themselves in a large white room, with one of the crew of the ship they had just gone to take over standing in the center.

"Hello. First off, do you guys have a name for your species? We haven't been able to call you anything specific."

"We are ourselves, we have no name as you would call it," one answered.

That wasn't very helpful.

"Oh well, regardless, I'm in charge of your ship now."

The aliens looked at each other. He had to be kidding them, right?

"And you're going to tell me all about whoever is in charge on your end.

This kid was not just funny, he was in fact hilarious.

"There is no way that is happening."

Jhe Darkshadow opened his eyes. "There is as of right now."

The aliens, who had never experienced an emotion like fear before, suddenly found someone adding it to their system like a batch of new code being swapped into a program. And when they learned of it, they found that they were, in fact, very afraid.

He pushed deep into their psyches and tore at their deepest and darkest memories, and none of them knew how to deal with what he did. None of them could do anything but submit.

The aliens fell over onto the floor, quivering slightly. Anya cheered, Ulysses nodded approvingly, and Aegenor grunted.

"Nice trap, but we haven't rigged their entire ship with copper floors."

"You're such a pessimist," Anya retorted.

"Realist."

"What next?" Ulysses asked.

Aladdin walked through the open door into the battleship and started flipping some switches.

"Do you even know what you're doing?" Aegenor asked.

"I ganked some of their memories about how to operate the ship's systems."

Anya looked uncomfortable, and Ulysses squeezed

her shoulder. Aladdin kept working. "And now the Cavalry arrives."

There was a rumble, and the sound of something else docking with the battleship.

"What exactly is that?" Ulysses said it like an order.

"The reinforcements I asked the Librarian to send. The four of us can't fly this thing ourselves. Anya, you're in charge of engineering. Ulysses comms, Aegenor security."

"And you are?" Aegenor asked, already knowing the answer.

Aladdin showed off his pearly whites. "Why, Aegenor, I'm your trusted captain."

There was another rumble.

"Was that another shuttle?" Anya pondered.

"No, that was Maximus. Explosives expert. You'll meet him. I doubt their security detail will be doing too well right about now."

"So, what, we just wait around while your Index thugs clean the place up?" Aegenor said, grimly.

"Of course not, we've got our part to do. Not that this should be too difficult."

The four of them found, as Anya sliced, Ulysses pounded, Aegenor shot, and Aladdin hacked their way through the ship, it really wasn't. Turns out aliens that have to grab your spine to control your mind are pretty ineffectual when you kill them.

* * * * *

The ship slipped through space, and carefully, without opening communication, they submitted their pass codes. Just as casually, they received a confirmation message. They were passing through, just as usual. Nothing odd about it to the fleet around them. They slid by, into the black space beyond the blockade, free to their next target.

Aegenor grimaced, "That should have been more complicated."

Aladdin shrugged. "Know your enemy."

Maximus was nearby, playfully tossing a grenade up and down and wearing his beige trench coat and bandoliers of explosives with the same level of grace as his finely trimmed beard.

"We ready to board yet?" The Rimward man asked, bored.

"You'll get to blow things up, I promise." Aegenor answered.

"I'd better."

The Baktun Bird, as Aladdin had christened it, slid in next to Memnor's ship and the two ships docked with a strange pseudo-organic coupling system that one couldn't help but think was a little bit dirty looking. The team stood ready, weapons brandished and eyes ahead.

Anya and Ulysses thought of their brothers and sisters they had left behind, the ones Memnor had tried to kill. Aladdin thought of Nightingale, and how proud she'd be of him leading an assault to take out one of The Emperors' Councilors. Aegenor thought of how little she cared about this anymore. Maximus thought of the maximum blast radius of a P-48b cluster bomb.

The seal was complete. Aladdin waited anxiously for the doors to open. They didn't.

"Oh frak," Aladdin's eyes got wide. "I made a mistake. I made a huge mistake."

Anya wanted to ask him what the mistake was, but as she started stumbling, she realized it herself. The design of these ships linked both organic and inorganic systems when they docked. The air was linked, and their ship's air was being pumped with knockout gas. They had planned to wear masks onto the other ship, but it was too late and the last thing Anya saw before she passed out was Aegenor limply reaching for Aladdin as though to crush his throat.

* * * * *

When Aegenor awoke, she was in a nice bed with a cup of tea next to it. She sat up and, ignoring the tea, stumbled out of bed woozily. The room was posh and as her bare feet walked through the fur carpet, the door opened to reveal one of the coiled aliens. She tensed.

"Calm yourself. I am Memnor, member of the Council of the Great Assimilation."

She tried to steady herself to look formidable. "You've been causing me a lot of trouble, mister Councilor."

The thing seemed to give an impression of a bow or a nod.

"As have you. But you are notable—more notable than your fellows in one regard."

"And what's that?"

"You aren't content with being who you are. You want to crush others and climb over their bodies on the way to the top." It seemed to be trying to mimic human mannerisms without quite understanding them, and the effect was disconcerting.

"That's a harsh way of putting it."

"But it's true. Would you allow me to show you something?"

Aegenor shrugged. "Sure, why the hell not?"

"It's not what you'd expect. I want to show you a memory."

"You mean jack into my mind."

"I do mean that."

Aegenor didn't take as long as she should have to debate it. "Sure, why the hell not?" She repeated.

It latched onto her spine, and she was galaxies away. There were planets beyond her counting filled with life, all part of one collective whole. They were united, strong, making leaps and bounds of unimaginable progress. It was glorious. And at the head of it all were the Emperors, and the Council, and Memnor. Each was a jewel in the crown that topped the body of an empire beyond the wildest dreams she'd ever had.

"Isn't it wonderful?" Memnor thought.

She could only agree.

* * * * *

She was dressed now, having eaten, and was being led through the hospital's clean hallways to see her fellows. Others of Memnor's kind slithered between cubicles, each holding someone she had seen on the ship. There were those dumb Hypercubes and the bomb man. She enjoyed seeing them knocked out, drugged up, and laid out on tables, things digging into their spines. "What are they doing to them?"

"Adding their memories to my database. I collect their memories, their wisdom, their life stories. I add them to my own. Through others, I have lived more lifetimes even than all The Emperors. I am a library of life, the re-incarnation of thousands of lives. And soon I will be a God."

Aegenor believed the thing, but couldn't see how it was possible.

It seemed to sense her uncertainty. "The Emperors have found the secret to immortality. I seek to emulate their success, and then surpass it. I think I have found the key in a pair of humans named Spinneret Jhe Sang Ki and Index Jade Darkshadow."

Aegenor narrowed her eyes, "Jhe? That's Aladdin's dad, then."

"You're correct." Memnor opened a door and Aegenor saw Aladdin strung up, nearly naked, tubes dug in all over his body and his spine lined with copper wires.

"Here is the son you speak of, and I have a way to get what I need out of him."

She looked at Aladdin's torso. He'd clearly been tortured, cut, beaten. "You're going to torture him more?"

"No, even worse. I'm going to tell him a story.

FILE 14:
MORDRED'S LULLABY

Memnor ran the talon-like end of its appendage along Aladdin Index's face. It was so odd, skin. Some of The Emperors and their soldiers had it, rather than segmented exo-skeletons, and Memnor had never really gotten used to it. But here was one right under Memnor's tendrils. The skin felt odd; it had too much give. Memnor pressed on it, and watched the skin rise back up, with some redness where the tendril had pushed down on it. Fascinating! The other one, Aegenor Index, kept moving her eyes back and forth in weird ways and had her head (was that the name of the uppermost body segment?) leaning down. Memnor recalled these as signs of discomfort in homosapiens.

"Are you alright, Aegenor Index?"

"Why do you always have to fucking say 'Index'?"

"That's your... House, Aegenor Index."

"House?"

"Is that translation incompatible?"

"I fucking think so."

"I comprehend. I will research your linguistics further." Memnor broke into her mind.

So until then, this will have to do.

Get out of my head! Memnor was filled with an emotion that was sort of like joy.

No. Now we are going to go into Aladdin Index's mind. We are going to have some fun with him, maybe we'll break him. Can you think of any good ways?

She looked at him with an expression of pain, or maybe just intense discomfort? Both? So much to learn! *Not really. He really hates that Jade Darkshadow lady.*

Indeed he does. And that is most relevant to my motives, Its tendrils coiled and shivered in a mix of anticipation and berserk fury.

Let me comb your mind. I need to find a story he can relate to...

No.

Memnor stabbed into her psyche and she screamed. It was an interesting reaction, but Memnor ignored it and dug through her memories, finding a story most appropriate.

It's story time Aegenor Index....

Aladdin awoke.

No, that wasn't right. Who was Aladdin? Mordred looked down at his hands. He'd dreamed he was... Well he hadn't looked English, that was for sure. But it was just a dream, and an odd one. There was a bird that was apparently an important bird...

The dream was fading fast, and Mordred couldn't hold onto it for longer than a few moments as the light of the dawn crept into his room. Then it hit him: it was dawn.

Mordred didn't waste any time getting out of his bed and putting his clothes on. Mother was not the kind of person one wanted to keep waiting. Moving as fast as he could manage silently, he fetched the water and fresh wood, stoked the stove, gathered fresh eggs and milk from the barn, and began to make Mother's breakfast. He could sense her moving down the steps—she made no sound but had a certain aura he had grown to recognize. He didn't even need to look to know she was wearing her jade-green dress, blonde hair running down her shoulders.

"Mordred, you're up early."

He was always up early, yet she always said that. Mordred sliced her bread, flipped the fried eggs over the slices just as she liked them, and placed the plate and milk at her place setting. She began eating, and after a few bites looked at him standing there, hands clasped in front, lips pursed.

"Oh, Mordred dear, get yourself something to eat. You don't have to wait like that."

He did have to wait like that. He'd seen what happened when he didn't. Mordred hastily scraped himself together some food and ate it, pacing himself carefully. It was very important that he finish eating at just about the same time as Mother. Mordred knew very well how life needed to be lived, and that was with the obedience of the stars to their constellations.

Every day was like every other. He performed the morning routine, and then his mother and he strolled into the woods and she began his training. Oaf was there (not his real name, but that was what Mother wanted Mordred to call him).

"Swing at him again, Mordred."

Mordred's panting was like dragon breath, rolling like steam through the cold, dark air of the dawning sun. He hefted the sword, which was intentionally heavier than it should be, and charged at Oaf. His calves were sore, his arms aching, and Oaf stood there in his painted black armor with a blunt sword hanging casually in his hand and eyes staring blandly out of the helmet. He swung, and Oaf almost halfheartedly deflected the blow, but Mordred kept swinging, angling, slicing and jabbing, trying to get a blow in edgewise. Oaf simply parried and dodged and retaliated. With every blow Oaf gave Mordred it grew harder to get back up, until his body refused to rise again.

"Another day of disappointment Mordred. I expected better today. Don't you want to make your mommy proud?"

Mordred tried to open his mouth to respond, but no words came out—just a moaning noise. His mother and Oaf walked off, their footsteps fading into the woods, and Mordred opened his bruised eyes to the sky. The bruises were thick. He was rarely given time enough to heal the wounds he sustained, which meant he always ached, always hurt, and never forgot the extent of his failure.

Someday he'd meet his scum of a father, and show him what he thought about him. Every beating he received was because of Arthur Pendragon. Every hateful day was his father's fault. And Mordred could not wait to spit in his face and take his kingdom from him. Mother Empress LeFey would be so pleased. He stared up at the trees as their leaves swayed gently in the sunlight, until suddenly his view was filled with a feminine mess of red hair and freckles.

"Mister are you alright?"

"Mrerrrngeneh," Mordred said.

"You look terrible! We need to get you out of here. I'll take you to my house, we'll clean you up."

"Mrehnenenenenenenn!"

"Don't worry you are going to be okay." He tried to protest, but he wasn't actually in any condition to protest anything about this situation, so the girl picked him up and started to carry him, slowly, through the woods. Mordred tried to struggle or speak, but all it did was make him pass out.

* * * * *

When Mordred awoke, he was staring at a thatched roof's interior and feeling very...balmy, in the sense that there was balm all over his body. He sat up and heard his bones creak as a few things popped (hopefully) back into place. He examined his meager surroundings, nothing like his own home. Bone-carved spoons rested in wooden bowls with the remains of gruel, sunlight rained down from holes in the roof into buckets. Mordred painfully slid his feet off the hay mattress and gritted his teeth as he pushed his body to stand up. He put his foot out in front of him, reaching for a step, and promptly fell over, his head making a nasty smack against the dirt floor. He rolled over again and started attempting to crawl. He heard the door swing open and looked up to see the redhead from before looking down at him, carrying what looked like food.
"Well you're never going to heal if you throw yourself on the floor repeatedly."
"Only the once."
She set the food down and gently helped him into a sitting position.
"Your wounds are serious, you can't..." She examined him and stopped, baffled. "Your wounds can't have healed that quickly. That's just impossible."
"I'm not better."
"A normal person would be in bed for weeks."
He tried to put on a grin. "Glad to be abnormal."

She ignored him and started trying to shove some porridge into his mouth.

"I don't want to eat it." He tried to bat the spoon away with all the coordination of a blind puppy. She landed a spoonful in his mouth and kept shoveling in more, so he relented and started chewing.

"You're lucky to be alive, you know, and that I know about stitching people up as well as I do."

Mordred looked her over. She didn't have the mannerisms of a peasant, but she dressed like one. "Who are you anyways?"

"Thought you'd never ask. Alice MacLeod."

Alice... That name rung a bell.

"My father Donovan used to be a Knight for Lord Carthage, but when the witch Morgan LeFey came through and exiled Carthage, my father decided to stay and lead the rebels against her. So we hide here in the woods."

Mordred just stared. She just kept talking.

"Someday King Arthur and his knights will hear of our plight and they will come, and we'll fight with them and free ourselves from their heinous grasp. We'll have freedom, and Morgan LeFey and her bastard Mordred will have their heads on pikes!"

Mordred nodded. "Oh, good! That's...very good. Okay. Yes."

She raised an eyebrow, "That was not a very enthusiastic or convincing whatever that was supposed to be."

Mordred thought on his feet. "My family works at the castle. As servants." It wasn't all lie. He was really a servant, even though Mother had so many of her own. "I don't want to get caught in the crossfire."

Alice nodded. "You were so close to the castle, I figured you had to have some sort of ties to it. Rest assured, when the people are free that will include your family. We know very well that Morgan keeps most of her servants there through coercion. We're leading a revolution for the people, not against them."

Mordred nodded, not entirely sure that made sense, but he was willing to roll with it.

"We're planning our revolt soon, so when it happens, be ready to get your family and friends to somewhere safe."

He nodded. She spoke more of revolution, and when he dreamed, he dreamed of her with a red flag, charging on horseback to cut his head off, and she was glorious.

"I don't think he's awake."

He's in the second level of dreaming, dreaming within dreaming. It's not entirely real to him, and we might bleed through, said the demon, clicking and slithering around his body.

"I'm not sure this is right."

You crossed this line, Aegenor Index. You can't jump back over it.

He awoke again to find himself alone in the forest where he had been picked up, his wounds bandaged and a small kerchief of bread and cheese next to him. Tucked inside was a piece of parchment.

"Dear Stranger:
We couldn't afford to keep you longer. Being from the castle, you would be a danger to both of us in our village. I wish you all the best, and await the day of freedom. – Alice"

Mordred wanted to rip it up, but he hid it in his tunic instead. When he walked into the castle, Morgan ran up to him all fury and flurry.

"Where have you been? I've been worried sick! No

one was there to make me breakfast even."

Mordred just kept walking to his room.

"Mordred!" she yelled, "MORDRED!"

* * * * *

Mordred panted as Oaf swung at him again, nimbly stepping to the side and letting the man's excessively large sword cut into the dirt next to him. Mordred put his foot on Oaf's sword before he could raise it up, and aimed his own sword at Oaf's throat.

"Very good, Mordred. Very good."

He looked over at his mother. That was the first time she had ever said a word of encouragement during these sessions, and he was so distracted that Oaf took the opportunity to punch him in the face.

Every day, he got better. Every day, he fought harder. His bruises turned to callouses, and his callouses turned to armor, and Jade smiled.

Aladdin staggered backwards. Jade? Mordred shook his head. Who was Jade? He saw visions of a strange life, and as Oaf charged towards him again, he steadied his hands on his sword. This time he wouldn't miss.

He didn't.

Morgan giggled. "You're ready, Mordred."

* * * * *

Alice sat in the tree, legs dangling, watching the chipmunk below her sniffing for food. The boy she'd rescued before had left her a note on her bedside table. She wondered why he hadn't talked then, but when he approached the tree through the brush, she waved excitedly. He was, after all, kind of cute.

"Alice? That you?"

"It's me! It's good to see you. You look better."

"I am better." He smiled at her, then averted her eyes as she dropped down from the trees to walk next to him. "I'm glad you came back. I wanted to see you again, but I didn't think you'd be able to get free to see me."

"Alice, there are some things I need to talk to you about."

"Like your name? You never mentioned that."

He looked at her sadly, like he was about to break her.

"You need to listen to me. Morgana is going to take on Arthur soon. She's going to start by slaughtering you and your rebels in the woods, as practice."

"What? How do you know all this?"

"The attack is going to come in three days. She's gathering her forces in the north. They'll be down here soon, rest, and then crush you."

"That's not much time."

"It's enough time for you to get out of here, and get your family out of here."

"Why are you telling me this?"

"Alice, I don't want you to die. You need to get out of here."

"And you're betraying everyone in the Castle why?"

"Because I hate everyone in the castle."

"Even your mother?"

"Especially my mother."

"You'll be killed if they learn it's you."

"I can live with that."

"Give me one reason to believe you. Why should I trust what you're telling me and move all of my family and allies out of here?" She looked him right in the eyes, and he put his hand on her shoulder.

"My name is Mordred."

She was silent as she looked at him again for the first time; his bruises, his face so similar to the dark Queen who had walked amongst them, his clothes too nice to be those of a servant. All the things she should have seen when she first found him lying in the woods but didn't because he was beaten and alone. Here was Mordred, whom she was sworn to kill, whom she had hated from the moment she had learned to hate, telling her to run. Looking at her with eyes like that. Alice did the only thing she could do then. She ran.

* * * * *

"I don't get what you're doing Memnor. I don't see how this does anything."

You don't?

"I don't."

What are stories to beings, Aegenor?

"They're stories. They're entertaining and frak."

No, they're who we are. They define us. They replicate throughout the ages, and they drive our cultures forward to new ideas, and remind us of old ones. Aladdin holds a bond with a being he shouldn't, a being who is dead, who should only have a bond with his father. Why is that, Aegenor?

Aladdin was breathing slowly hooked up to the dreaming machine, the wires connecting his spine to Memnor's tendrils were quivering slightly. Aladdin looked like some sort of cyberpunk crucifix, his arms splayed out, pumped with drugs and sedatives.

"Because Aladdin is more like his father than his siblings. He's close enough that there is some sort of tie that Jade can latch onto."

Precisely. And this story is his. Whatever he sees in it,

he's willing to follow this story to its end.

What does that mean? It's just a story."

It means I can dig into his mind through the story without him noticing. As he falls into the story, I can seep through the layers he doesn't want me to see, and dig through his secrets. And I've learned a lot already. With every page of the story he turns, he gives me more. He made Jade into Morgan.

"I thought that was you." Aegenor wasn't exactly sure what sort of expressions a coil plate alien was capable of, but she didn't really like the look of how it quivered then.

I just set the story. He casts the roles. Meanwhile, I've been able to cut through his defenses and pull out his memories of Jade Darkshadow, and how she haunted him. I've learned quite a bit about how she is still tied to this universe. Things I can use. Things that will change everything.

Its tendrils swirled through the air. If she could guess, maybe it was excited.

"So you're done? You got what you needed?"

What you need you never quite know until the story is done.

* * * * *

Morgan LeFey was proud to be at the flank of her army, proud to see Mordred and Oaf at the front of it. They were parading to the village of those pesky rebels ready to crush them, slaughter them, and bring on the end of Lady Carthage's pitiful insurrection. Then she would kill kind king Arthur, take his throne, take his crown, and be the Queen of the Britons she always should have been. That was her plan, it was what she intended, it was what she had so long hoped and dreamed, and all of a sudden it came crashing down when she saw banners in the woods and a long line of knights and pikemen.

"Morgan!" Arthur yelled through the trees. "Your surprise has been had, and I can't say it was a very good one."

Morgan screamed in anger, gnashed her teeth, tugged at her hair, and raged into the mist that was beginning to fill the forest.

Mordred looked at Arthur through the mist and began to trot his horse forward, ahead of his troops. Oaf began to follow, but Mordred held his hand out and no one followed. Arthur, likewise, rode out to greet him.

"Hello, dad. I'm Mordred."

Arthur looked at him, disappointment reigning in his gaze. "You're leading an army against the free peoples of Britain. You could have been so much more."

"Well, this was all really my mom's idea. I'm not quite into it, in all honesty."

Arthur looked surprised.

"Seriously, I don't really see why we should be fighting at all right now. I'd rather this whole war thing just went by the wayside. But I'm sure mother dearest wouldn't approve of that."

"Mordred!" She yelled, cutting through the ranks of troops, her face the snarl of an angry panther. "What are you doing? Get back here and rally your troops."

"Actually, mother Empress, I don't think I will."

"That's an order! Listen to your mother."

"You're not my mother," he declared, squinting at her across the mists. "And this isn't how the story goes."

"This isn't a story little one!"

Aladdin just laughed. "Of course it is. It couldn't be anything else. Now get back into character. I'm about to break the fourth wall."

Arthur backed up his horse a few steps. The armies looked confused, and Jhe Aladdin began to tell them a story.

The Littlest Memnor
by Jhe Aladdin

Memnor was born on a world so far away from ours that if you looked up at night, you couldn't see a single star from our own sky. It was a sad little Memnor sitting in its hole.

"No it's not!" said Memnor. "I'm a proud Memnor."

But the story didn't care, because Memnor was stupid and had linked its central nervous system into Aladdin's head. Memnor had always been stupid. It had been a stupid little Memnor ever since Admiral Moloch put his big metal boots down on Memnor's planet and claimed it in the name of the Emperors and their Council and their dubiously Great Assimilation. Memnor had thought it was clever, had thought it had played its way up the chain, had thought it was going to be important, but Memnor didn't want to understand the truth; that Memnor was always destined to be insignificant. No matter what Memnor did, it could never escape the fact that it was climbing up a high ladder, trying to take the spot of the big man at the top who could kick the ladder down at any time.

So Memnor thought it would be clever, and decided it would go get its own ladder. Memnor asked around, and it was told that Jade and Kalingkata would know how to get a ladder. So Memnor, who was too afraid to ask them what was what, decided to go behind their backs to steal their friend's memories.

It wasn't a coincidence Memnor was named Memnor. Even though Memnor liked to think that was always its name, or its name was fate, it couldn't deny the fact that its name had been dreamed up by an Emperor over half a bottle of Scotch and a dry pastry.

"What does it do?" Moloch asked.

"Well it messes with people's memories," the Emperor stuttered through the alcohol.

"Well, should we give it a name? We're going to put it on the Council, right?"

"Memory bot!" The Emperor shouted.

"That's stupid," Moloch retorted.

"Johnny Mnemonic?"

"Mnemnon?"

"Memnor!" The Emperor settled on.

See, that was the thing that Memnor never liked to admit. It was always just a cog in other beings' plans, thinking it was king of the hill when really it had been given an anthill built on the dust of the hill it originally wanted to climb.

Memnor looked up at the stars and saw strange ones. It looked around and saw opportunity, and forgot about the lies it had convinced itself were true. In the grand scheme of the universe, there were billions of stars and only one small, dark, deluded Memnor; friendless even amongst its own kind, deathly afraid of being anything more than it could be, and on a never-ending quest to be that.

But what Memnor really should have anticipated, and made itself aware of, was that it wasn't as in control of things as it thou—

Memnor screamed, or Aegenor thought it screamed. Aladdin's eyes were open, and he was looking at her though his bloodshot focus with a sly smirk on his face. He'd known what Memnor was doing?

You're wrong. I knew what was going on, and I know

how to be immortal. I can be a God.
Aladdin just stared at Memnor, and it slithered away.

"Aegenor," Aladdin muttered weakly. "I know what he's going to suggest, and you don't want to do it."

"I can do whatever I want, Jhe Aladdin," she spat.

"This isn't some one-upmanship Aegenor. What Memnor wants to do, you'll regret for the rest of your life."

The blood was dry from the torture, and Aegenor's eyes were dry from her sadness. She laughed.

"It is one-upmanship. This is all about being better, about getting a foot up from where I used to be. You little selfish prick. You think you're so special, being handed everything you've ever gotten on a nice golden platter."

"Who I am doesn't change what Memnor wants to do."

"When I'm better then you, Jhe Aladdin. Visibly better, not just on the inside. You'll regret trying to tell off." She turned triumphantly and walked for the door as Aladdin shook his head ever so slightly.

"No, I won't regret it at all."

She ignored his last words, which was fitting being that Aegenor would never hear Aladdin speak again.

* * * * *

She was on the road to success. She was a triumph. She was a queen. She was the winner. Jhe Aladdin, with all he had thought he was bringing to bear on the world, was in fact no one when compared to the utter wonder of Aegenor Valor. Her head was held high as she walked next to Memnor, who crept along the floor. Whatever was next, she was prepared. She had chosen her side, and the future was ready to begin.

"Aegenor, the plan is now nearing its completion. The fool of a boy is wrong. I know how to achieve immortality, and I wish for you to help me with the first step."

"Okay, what do I have to do?"

"Just stand there," Memnor said as it coiled up her leg.

FILE 15:
THE LAST MIND IN THE HALLWAY

Imagine your whole life is a hallway lined with doors. Every door you choose to walk through connects to a hallway with more doors, each connecting to hallways with more doors, and you walk on and on until you die.

Now imagine you reach a hallway with no doors except the one you've just closed behind you, and you hear the lock click. There is nowhere to go. You have made your last choice, because from this point on, who you were is dead.

This is where the story of Aegenor Valor ends. This isn't where she dies. This is far worse than that.

Aegenor awoke in a hallway filled with locked doors, marked with strange black dripping symbols. Were they doors? When she stepped close to them they felt like holes, and her feet felt like stumbling...but they weren't quite feet. Were they? They were partially feet. They were not quite attached to legs. They were somewhat snakes.

They were somewhat her own. They were somewhat God's. She felt sickness, and ten dozen emotions she had never thought of feeling; things she couldn't find words for, things she had known before when she was...

She screamed, but it felt like an experiment. It felt like something she had felt before. She had screamed before. She had screamed when Wesley Viper stabbed her in the leg and told her to get on her knees as the blood gushed down her leg. She had screamed when she'd gotten drunk and accidentally shot her friend Vienna in the head while waving her gun around.

It was only then that Aegenor realized those memories weren't just hers anymore; and neither were the eyes she used to see them with.

Let go, Aegenor. This will be so much better than you can ever expect. I know what I'm doing. I can make us powerful. Let go.

Aegenor shook her head and tried to keep pushing down the hallway. "No. No I don't want this."

I am better than you. I deserve your body, Aegenor, and I need it. This is the grand experiment. This is immortality. This is Godhood.

She felt the memory of eating ice cream for the first time at the Index; how it tasted, how it felt in her mouth. She remembered the boy who had bought it for her...what was her name?

Aegenor suddenly realized this had never been about a partnership. This had been about Memnor needing to be the Emperor, and Memnor thinking Aegenor was strong enough physically and weak enough mentally to be a good host. Suddenly, Aegenor started feeling okay with this, which made her panic, because the only way she could ever be okay with that was if she was losing herself, like tears falling into a river. She tried to crawl down the hallway, but she was already in the room with no doors, and she realized far too late that Aegenor Valor wasn't a human being anymore. She realized too late that she was, in fact, a new dress.

Then she stopped realizing anything at all.

* * * * *

Memnor had seen suns die in the memories of ancient beings. It had lived for millennia in its short decades of life, and it had thought that memory could compare favorably to experience, but Memnor had no idea before how wrong it was. Its body was on the floor, sterile and dead, crumpled up, a few of its tendrils awkwardly hanging from Memnor's new spine. Spine! Memnor had a spine! Oh that was interesting, wasn't it?

Oh God, please let me out of here, please let me out. Aegenor screamed in her head.

Memnor was amazed she could still exert that much control over her body. After all, she was quite the weakling when it came to her mind. But this was her body. Memnor then realized its mistake: her spirit and body were tied together, so Memnor couldn't kick her out. He had to make her a part of itself permanently.

"Come here," Memnor whispered. "In a few seconds you won't even feel bad about what I've done to you."

Aegenor screamed and screamed, but Memnor knew better than she did. And soon, there was neither.

* * * * *

Aegamemnor woke up. She was suddenly aware of herself. She wasn't...who she was before. Memnor and Aegenor were different people, certainly, and so was she.

206

She felt like them—both of them, and yet neither of them. Aegamemnor stood up and flexed her hand. It felt odd to flex a hand instead of a tendril, and yet it was also the most normal thing in the world. She didn't have tendrils anymore, but she had seen the stars.

Memnor had been rather evil – evil...that was something Memnor wouldn't have said – but it had also had the right end goal. Being on the Council was the goal, and then becoming God King Emperor of the universe. Aegamemnor thought how odd it was that Memnor had wanted to live forever through her, and how Aegenor had not wanted a part in this at all, and how both of them were gone now. No one had gotten what they wanted. There had been a long hallway filled with two minds, one chasing down the other like prey, but the hunt killed them both. The last mind in the hallway was neither the prey nor the predator, but the child of their lust and fear. The one to open up the room with no doors and step out into her own mind. She was Aegamemnor, and oh did she lust.

FILE 16:
ROLLER DERBY QUEEN

Anya Hypercube woke up to see Aegenor staring at her face, but there was something wrong with Aegenor. She didn't quite look like her, even though she did. It was nothing physical, it was her...demeanor. The way she carried herself and the glint in her eyes.

"Hello Anya. It's interesting seeing you."

"Aegenor." Anya tried to move and felt the restraints keeping her down. "Aegenor, you have to help me get up. We have to get out of here and find my brother and Aladdin." She kept looking into Aegenor's eyes.

"I'm not Aegenor anymore, Anya. I'm...actually that's a good question. My mind is that of Aegenor, and of Memnor, combined. It's rather interesting, but really kind of psychotic when you think about it. But I suppose that means the psychotic is in me as well."

Anya wasn't sure what to say to that. She wasn't even quite sure what it meant. "You can't just put people's minds in other people's bodies!"

"I think you of all people should know that's not true."

"What in Bowie's name are you talking about?"

Aegenor tilted her head to the side. "Really? You don't know? Memnor would have told you, but frankly you probably wouldn't want to know. Regardless, the point is that I am very definitely the minds of Aegenor and Memnor now."

And you know what? They both deserved to lose themselves. Here I am, and you're going to listen to me.

She thought she heard the last words in her head. It had to just be an illusion.

It's not.

Anya looked at what had once been her friend in horror. She hated having people probe her mind, and Aegenor doing it was somehow even worse, because of course, it wasn't really Aegenor.

"Let her go. Get out of her head!"

"There's nothing to let out. I'm a new me now. I'm no one you remember. I should get a new name. Though I suppose an old one would work as well. What about something evocative?"

"Jerk face?" Anya suggested.

"Aegamemnor!" She exclaimed. "Reminds me of that old king from the Iliad. I will be a queen, so it fits. Goodbye, Anya Hypercube. I'd like you to come work for me and help to create my new empire, but I see you have some reservations, so I'll leave you to your thoughts.

Anya pulled against the restraints. Whatever had happened to Aegenor, no matter how abrasive she had been, she didn't deserve it. No one deserved that. Anya needed to get out and find Aladdin. Immediately.

Aegamemnor went back to her room, or what had been her room. It seemed homely and the furniture didn't fit her body, but she soon started realizing her body had other needs—like hunger. She wanted food, and though she remembered how good copper used to taste, she also knew her new body wouldn't take to it very well. Aegamemnor walked over to the confiscated object room and struggled for a moment figuring out how to open the door. She had no tendrils, so she had to project her thoughts at it and sort of shove the controls at the same time. The door slid open, and she started looking through the bags until she found some apples and granola bars. She bit into an apple and remembered taste. It was glorious, and she felt...human.

Aegamemnor suddenly remembered something she desperately wanted to know, something simple, and ran to get it from Anya Hypercube. She barreled through the door, a granola bar still hanging out of her mouth, and put her hands on the copper tubes she used to put her tendrils into. That did nothing, and she felt quite silly for thinking it would. She bit off the chunk of granola and began chewing it as she focused her mind; this whole non-contact thing was strange, but it functioned.

Anya? Am I in your mind?

"Get the hell out!"

Excellent! I need you to think back, to when you were outside with Aladdin. I want to see that memory.

"No."

Aegamemnor shrugged. She would find it anyway, it would just be more difficult without Anya's cooperation. Memnor dug into Anya's brain, as her eyes rolled back in her head.

"Jade!" Aladdin screamed, "Not again! Never again!" but Aegamemnor ignored him and closed her eyes. She had a memory she wanted to relive.

* * * * *

Anya enjoyed having extra people around the house. Not because the house was ever really silent, but eventually you get used to the seeing the same fifteen people every day. She wandered off, and found Aladdin alone on the lawn, looking up at the sprawling sky shining through the high glass dome.

"What are you doing out here? Everyone is inside."

Aladdin gestured for her to come closer, so she did and popped a squat next to him.

"Your house is bugged." He tossed her what looked like a listening device someone had fried.

"Oh my God."

"Don't worry about it, I've been being followed since I got this assignment. Hexie sent someone to keep track of me, and obviously they need to keep detailed reports. But that won't last."

"I don't see why not."

"Because we aren't going to stay here. I'm tired of playing by everyone's rules. I'm tired of waiting around while other people dictate what I do, where I run. So I'm going to run, and I'm going to take out these people who are trying to kill your family."

"Then I'm coming with you, which means also Ulysses."

Aladdin just shook his head.

"I can't have you guys tailing me around. I mean..."

Anya put her hand on his shoulder.

"If it were your sister, would you sit back and wait?"

Aladdin put his own hand on her shoulder. "Not for a moment."

"Then I'm coming."

Aladdin just smiled, "Anya, do you see all those stars?"

"Of course I do. There's Orion's belt. I always love finding that one. Wherever I am, if I can find it, I feel safe."

"Any reason behind that?"

"When I was a kid, my dad, Geraldine, and whichever of us kids who were born by then would sit out on the lawn and look at the stars together, all as a family. Whenever I see it, even if I'm alone, I know that the same stars are there for them. So I'm never really alone."

"That's why we're going to win."

"I don't follow."

"When those things that attacked us look up at the stars, they don't see the same ones. Not just different constellations, but totally different stars. They're too far away to see those stars with eyes, so when they look up to see the light that shows them home, that they're loved, it isn't there. Every night, we have our stars above our heads, and they can only look at the blackness in between for comfort."

Anya hadn't expected that sort of answer. She hadn't been sure what to expect.

That was when they heard Aegenor crying. She was on her knees, arms crossed, weeping, her body pulsing with the sobs. Aladdin and Anya stepped over and asked if she was okay, tried to put their arms around her and comfort her, but she threw them off.

"I don't need anybody, and I don't want anybody, I just don't want to be alone."

She ran off into the night, and Anya and Aladdin stood dumbfounded.

* * * * *

Anya Hypercube strained against the straps. She had all sorts of gizmos in her mechanical limbs, but apparently the aliens had found all of them when they read her mind and wisely disabled her limbs. So she was straining with only half her body, and the other limbs were just weighing her down. It was frustrating, but not quite so frustrating as finally realizing how she could get out of her straps and then promptly getting rescued—which was exactly what happened.

The crisp sound of a few slices and the soft thud of Carnival Reichenbach drifted down the hallway, then a woman careened through on roller blades – wearing a plaid skirt, black turtleneck, black army jacket, goggles, large headphones and knee socks with kittens on them – and tore through Memnor's people with a katana.

You wanna see me gnash 'em
Slice 'em Gut 'em Cut 'em?
I'm a samurai of the 51st Baktun
Gunna arbitrate, castrate, violate, violent
With my arbitrary justice, bring the violins!

As the violins started playing from the headphones the lady was wearing, Anya watched sprays and spirals of black ichor fly across her field of vision. Eventually the woman came to a halt in front of Anya's chamber, spit out a piece of gum and, with her ichory fingers, popped in another.

"You Anya Hypercube?"

Anya suddenly realized that she could still trigger the emergency release on her arm and leg, which would have been more obvious had she not been drugged and captured.

"Yeah, I'm Anya. Just give me a minute, I'm almost out..."

The woman made several quick cuts, faster than eyesight, and the restraints fell free.

"Come on."

"Who are you?"

"Backgammon Jenny. I work for Aladdin's dad, and we're about to mount the mother of all rescue mission/assassination attempts. You ready to roll?"

Anya turned her limbs back on and got up shakily as they booted up. "Yeah, I'm ready."

Jenny nodded, and Anya wished she could have seen the eyes behind those goggles, but instead she saw only her own face, marred by the shining blots of ichor that dripped down the goggles.

"Then let's go. I'm not done killing people, and we have a lot of people to rescue."

"Is Ulysses okay?"

"We'll get him." Jenny looked at Anya more seriously than she had been looked at before in her life. "After we get Aladdin."

Anya didn't argue. The two of them were a flurry of death and cuts. The coiling aliens either fought or ran, but all of them fell to slices from Jenny's katana or Anya's bladed nails. Anya's hands cut through the bends in the aliens with fine precision, and her arm tired with the extremely fine dexterity she had to use to line up the hits, all while dodging their striking talons and lashing tendrils. She got cut a few times, but she left her foes gushing ichor on the floor. Not like Jenny's targets, though.
Jenny didn't use effort. Jenny wasn't fighting; she was killing. She was a one woman execution squad on roller blades, and anything that got in her way was dead. Bits of

coil flew against the wall and ichor pumped bubbling from their wounds.

Backgammon Jenny wasn't like her boss. Her boss had given up being a badass for suits and diapers. Backgammon Jenny rollerbladed up the cylinder walls of the hallway so she could slice through her foes from the ceiling. Jenny flipped through the air and kicked her suddenly sharp rollerblades to cut up some punk aliens that were in her way, and her sword never stopped its work. Backgammon Jenny was a punk. She had a gospel of Rock 'n' Roll intoxication and bloodshed.

Anya did her best to keep up and pull her own weight, but the truth was Jenny was a devout girl and she was going to church. By the time they reached Aladdin's room, the floor was slick with ichor and Anya wasn't sure if the dumb ship could even have much crew left. Jenny slid to a halt, popped her gum, and opened the door to reveal...nothing. There was no one there but a bunch of empty shackles.

Well shit," Jenny said, and just stared for a moment. "I hate it when rescue missions start getting ahead of schedule."

Jenny reached into her jacket and pulled out a weird looking cube that looked like it was alien tech, but also human tech—some sort of Hybrid. Anya would love to study it.

"What's that?"

"Ever play Backgammon?"

"Once or twice?" It better not be just a fancy looking doubling cube, she thought, though she noticed it had no numbers on it.

"It's a doubling cube."

Oh.

"Only this little buddy raises the stakes on your soul."

Carl Fredrickson

* * * * *

Jhe Aladdin hated having people in his mind. He'd had plenty of that as a child, and he wasn't about to take any more of it, thank you very much. Worse, though, was that Aegenor had let Memnor into her mind, not knowing the consequences. Aladdin ran barefoot across the floor of the spaceship, the weird metallic flesh of the ship feeling cold but mushy, yet also hard. He ran silently. Occasionally he encountered one of the aliens that ran the ship. Usually Aladdin would have been able to sneak by them with no problem, and some he did, but his injuries slowed him a bit. When one did spot him, he avoided the talon and got wrapped up in the rest of it so he could jam the scalpel he'd taken from the room between one of the alien's segments. The method cut him up more, but it killed the things. At least, he thought so. After he split them in two, the halves just sort of thrashed and screamed, and Aladdin didn't stick around to see if anyone came to help.

Aladdin ran, his legs burning, but he knew where he was going. While Memnor was in his head, he'd sneaked a thin peek for himself just to see the layout of the ship. Aladdin knew exactly where to go.

* * * * *

Aegamemnor puzzled at its old office. The furniture wasn't designed for her to sit in, obviously, and so wasn't very comfortable. If Memnor was in control, it would want to hop to a new body, and if Aegenor was in control, she'd want Memnor out as well. But neither of them were in charge now, were they?

Aegamemnor sat down awkwardly on a squishy cylinder she knew was meant to comfortably coil around.

216

It was strange. She was in charge, on the Council, working for the Librarian...but always friendless. In all her memories, no matter who she was, she was always alone. Aegamemnor looked around her old room and listened to the screaming in her head from the voices she used to be.

She would be better than them. Memnor was a fool and so was Aegenor. Aegamemnor would trump both of them, because she had both of their experiences and could see that both of them had lived meaningless lives. Aegamemnor would rule the universe...

But she would need people on her side to do that. Just then, an opportunity arose to give it a shot.

Jhe Aladdin stood before Aegamemnor, shirtless, shoeless, bloody, ichory, and holding a scalpel. He grimaced.

Memnor. Get out of her head."

"Memnor is gone. So is Aegenor before you ask. I'm me now."

"So you're a combined consciousness?" He seemed to inspect her, like he could see her souls through her clothing or something.

"Yes, call me Aegamemnor."

"The idiot who burned a thousand ships?"

"The sacker of Troy."

"I know a Troy, he's a nice guy. Not too bright though."

"So easy to sack."

"Paris would be unhappy to hear that."

"Paris is being sacked right now by my agents. Well, that and carpet bombed. You know, I didn't understand this before I had a body with a gender system, but you are attracted to that revolutionary girl in your memories, aren't you? Nightingale?"

Aladdin pointed the scalpel, still dripping ichor, at her

as though it was something far more deadly. "You shut up about her."

"You know, I have the memories of countless beings. Many from Earth. Did you know her mother is dying there according to medical records we stole?"

He sneered. "You looked that up just to taunt me?"

She shrugged.

"I didn't have to. It's all in my head, ready to be pulled out a moment's notice. I am a library, Aladdin. The knowledge of Memnor with the practicality of Aegenor. I know a lot of things. I know that you haven't even told your little lovebird you love her, you haven't even kissed her. She's still out of your reach. And she doesn't even feel the same way? And deep deep down you know that. You're coated in blood and she doesn't care—"

"She's fighting right now too! For something greater than herself!"

"And it will always be greater then you, won't it Aladdin? No matter what happens, whether you win the war or lose it, she'll never be done with her cause."

Aladdin was circling her, seething with rage, his bleeding feet still moving with the careful footwork of a professional Snowcutter. Not bad for a seventeen year old. Aegamemnor prepared to go to the next room over, though. Aladdin wouldn't mind.

"She will be done when Earth is free. We can be together. I can wait for that. She's worth it."

Aegamemnor just smiled and sent a thought to the wall computer. "When Earth is free, she'll have to help rebuild. She'll take up some sort of responsibility there. That's just who she is, and she still won't have time for you."

"I'll be there. We can be a partnership."

"You're a fool. I know things. She's never shown

romantic or sexual interest in anyone, ever. Its simply not in her make-up. Even if she had, there are better suited partners for her. That boy who broke her out of prison, Jack. Or David, who watches over her now while you gallivant around for a glorified sadist. She won't want you, the Librarian's little lapdog."

Aladdin heard the machinery in the wall start to hum. He wasn't sure whether to turn and look or keep his eyes focused on Aegamemnor, so he kept walking so he could see both...which gave Aegamemnor the chance to spring towards the swiftly rising wall. Aladdin cursed and charged after her. Behind the office was a series of very thin catwalks over what looked like molten copper. Aladdin tried hard not to roll his eyes that Memnor had a secret door to the food storage area. It was a giant fondue pot of metal, and Aegamemnor suddenly realized she wasn't in Memnor's coiled form and traversing this would be more dangerous for her than for Aladdin.

The metal was hot under Aladdin's feet, but he paced forward slowly.

"You don't have any rights to my memories. And you may know my dreams and my thoughts, but you don't know Nightingale. She's the best woman I've ever met, she's a hero, she's brave, and I'd die for her. I don't care that she'll never reciprocate what I feel. I don't expect her to." He stared her in the eyes. "She's worth believing in. And it's worth fighting for a place where people like her can live. I'm just sorry I couldn't save Aegenor. But now that she's gone, there's nothing I can do about that."

Aegamemnor shrugged, "Well, there is one thing you can do to prove your love for Nightingale. Do what the rest of your friends have been doing! Die for a cause."

Aegamemnor ran at Aladdin, and he slashed at her, but she blocked the strike with her metal arm. She kneed him, and he took the blow while jamming the scalpel into her forearm with a surgeon's precision. Her hand went limp as the scalpel surged with electricity, and he let go, cursing. She punched him, and he rolled forward with it, and dug his teeth into her cheek. She hadn't expected that.

Fine, she thought, we'll do this the old fashioned way. Aegamemnor took a deep breath and plunged her mind into Aladdin's.

Aladdin's mind, when entered without the guise of a story, was like something out of a dream. Aegamemnor stood in a landscape made entirely of the colors black and white—no shades in-between. White rivers with black lines showing their borders. Black dirt that blended together until you kicked up individual granules. There stood Aladdin, in color.

"Welcome, Aegamemnor, to my mind. You think you're so clever but—"

Aegamemnor screamed and fell to the floor, clutching the bleeding hole in her head where there used to be an eye. Aladdin turned to see Backgammon Jenny standing there, goggles up, looking coldly down at Aegamemnor with a shocked Anya standing not too far behind her.

"Aladdin, go with Anya. You two get the rest of the prisoners free and get us back onto your ship."

"Jenny, she—"

"Aladdin, shut up." She looked into his brown eyes with a cold fervor, and he stepped back. "I made your dad a promise long ago that I'd protect you."

Aegamemnor screamed, her blood dripping into the copper bellow, sizzling.

"And that includes doing the things you never should have to do. Like what I'm about to. Things you shouldn't have to live with."

"Jenny, we could save her somehow."

"You know better than I do that we can't. You met Jade."

Aladdin nodded.

Anya looked between them. "You're going to execute Aegenor?"

Aladdin walked away. "Aegenor, is dead Anya. You're just looking at her shell. She would have hated being someone else's puppet. She wasn't nice, but she deserved better than this, and her soul deserves some rest."

Anya bit her lip.

Aegamemnor tried to sit up. "I have the wisdom of tens of thousands of years! You can't just kill me."

Aladdin turned around. "Jade made that same sort of deal, and now she's living it up inside a battleship, causing more pain, when she should be dead. We deserve better than the kind of help you'd give." Aladdin turned again, and started walking out. "She was my friend. And you killed her. And I'm tired of that."

Anya looked at Aegamemnor, still holding a hand to her bleeding eye socket. Aegamemnor had started to laugh. Anya walked away without looking until she was out of the room. She and Aladdin heard the sound of steel being pulled out of a sheath, and then silence.

* * * * *

Aladdin and Anya got Ulysses out, then Maximus, then the rest of the crew. The Index troops were understandably unhappy about having tendrils attached to their spines, and also about being held prisoner in general.

"Is everyone mostly okay?"

There was a grumbling of concurrence.

"We need to wrest control of the ship from the remaining troops on board. Will that be a problem?"

The Index troops responded in quick succession.

"In Bowie's name, let's just get on with it."

"I don't worship Bowie."

"He's a prophet, not God."

"I'm Jewish."

"Well shut up, I'm a Pagan."

"And I don't believe in any of your shit."

"SHUT UP!"

Aladdin looked over at Ulysses and smiled in approval.

"Thank you, Mr. Hypercube. Now, I don't care where you're from, or what you're doing. We need to work together to take over this ship, for the sake of staying alive and also getting paid."

"So what do we have to do?"

"Kill or capture the rest of the crew."

"Do we have to do it with so much diversity?"

Bowie's bow tie, was he really having this conversation?

"Yes, we really have to do it with so much diversity. As of right now the Baktun Bird has the Interfaith Diversity Murder-Squad as its crew, so go live up to its name."

Aladdin raised his fist in the air and just yelled. It seemed like the thing to do. They yelled back, or maybe cheered. He wasn't sure. Either way, apparently the easiest way to control a mob of people who disagree with each other was to give them a name, tell them to kill some people, and then yell like a howler monkey. He'd have to remember that.

"Interfaith Diversity Murder-Squad? Really?" Anya muttered.

"I was thinking on my feet."

"If you ever want new feet, I can hook you up with improvements."

Anya and Aladdin laughed, and the Interfaith Diversity Murder-Squad walked off to live up to their name.

FILE 17:
THE DOUBLING CUBE

A doubling cube is used in the game of backgammon to raise the stakes of the game. Players take turns using it to raise the bet, first by 2, then 4, 8, 16, 32, 64, etc. Backgammon Jenny made her gamble. She turned the cube and doubled her wager.

When the last bits of Aegenor heard, "She was my friend," come out of Aladdin's mouth, the confusion and sorrow she felt was inexpressible. She strained at the edges of Aegamemnor's brain, and Aegamemnor was surprised it was Aegenor who could reach from the depths of her psyche rather than Memnor. But Aegamemnor didn't dwell on the curiosity, because she was about to die.

Backgammon Jenny snapped her goggles down over her eyes and lined her sword up with Aegamemnor's neck. Aegamemnor laughed and closed her one eye, listening to her own blood hiss as it dripped into the molten copper below. She thought of all her life could have been, and never had been. Somewhere in the back of her head,

Memnor panicked and Aegenor cried, and Aegamemnor could only see the hilarity of the whole thing. I mean, she was just born, impossibly old, and about to die! All those dreams of Godhood were ridiculous in hindsight. All those glories that should have been were only memories, and her memories were only as real as the story of her creation: a saga of betrayal, failure, malice, and idiocy that climaxed in the existence of her mind.

She felt the whoosh of the sword swing up and she laughed as the blade fell...and then stopped an inch from her face. She stopped laughing and looked up and Backgammon Jenny, who stared down cold and blank. Aegamemnor started to speak, but Jenny shoved the butt of the sword into her mouth and placed a single finger over her own thoughtfully.

"So, you're a combined being now, like Jakata was with Jade and Kalingkata. I never have had the pleasure before. What's it like in there, crowded?" She pulled the sword butt from Aegamemnor's mouth to let her answer.

"It's just me in here now."

"A pity. Are you sure?"

"The other voices that make me up are fading into oblivion."

"Not a pity, then. I was worried I'd come all this way for nothing." Jenny began wiping her sword off on her skirt. "Tell me then. The memories of Memnor are now in Aegenor's brain—"

"My brain."

"Whatever. They're in this body's brain permanently?"

"They're mine now."

"Awesome sauce." Jenny reached into her coat and pulled out a cube that looked like alien tech. First it was blank, but then one by one the numbers 2, 4, 8, 16, 32, and 64 began to appear on it. "Looks like my bet's about to pay off."

Jenny seemed to focus, and the cube began to glow with swirling energy. Jenny reached out and touched Aegamemnor's head. She tried to lean back from it, but couldn't, and soon there were four people in the room. Not the room they had been in—a different one. Memnor, Aegenor, Jenny, and Aegamemnor herself, who looked like a strange amalgam of her 'parents' in this place, all standing on what looked like a spider web. Jenny was crawling on it.

"Welcome to my mind," she said. "I hope you enjoy it here. But not all of you will be staying long:"

"Indeed they won't. Only I'll be walking out of here," Aegamemnor chided.

"You can't let me die," Memnor moaned. "I have the knowledge of eons, of dying stars and the path of galaxies."

"I am you. None of that dies," Aegamemnor snapped back.

Jenny squinted at them. She needed to play this right, and carefully.

"Aegenor, do you know who I am?"

Aegenor seemed startled that she was being asked to speak.

"Of course. You're Backgammon Jenny, right hand lady of the Spinneret."

"Quite right. But you don't really know me. Now, Aegenor, you're going to be walking out of here with your own body, and we'll be killing these other two. How does that sound?"

"I want them gone."

Jenny flashed her teeth. "Then this should be fairly simple."

Aegamemnor didn't know what this woman thought she could do. She'd never seen Jenny's memories.

"So, Memnor," Jenny said. "Let's get you out of the way." Jenny breathed out white sulfur, and the air stank of mint. She delved into memory and pulled at thought.

Memnor was a young creature in its coil hole, before it became Memnor. It was simply another coil then, and like the other coils it shared its memories freely, for they were all part of the larger whole. There was no one, only the us, and Memnor felt safe. Memnor had forgotten what it was like to not have a name, to be part of the larger whole rather than above it. It had lived so long in the minds of others that it had forgotten its own...and now it didn't even have that.

"No!" Aegamemnor cut in, wiping the memory away as they stood within the heart of a moon made nearly entirely of gallium, melting beneath the fingertips of the mercenary expedition that Memnor had taken the memories of.

"You can't separate him. If he starts being himself, I stop being."

"But I am myself."

Jenny exuded warmth and the planet began melting and collapsing in on itself, drowning them in liquid metal.

"You are only the combination of parts that make your whole."

"And what combination of parts are you, Jenny? You're no more than a King's fool and a babysitter." Jenny was right next to Aegamemnor then, and ran her fingers through her hair. Aegenor watched cautiously.

"I am the daughter of a fool and the apprentice to a Wizard. I am a punk rock graffiti queen samurai on rollerblades. I am anyone I want to be. I'm Morgan Le Fey, I'm your dead cat, I'm Backgammon Jenny, and you'd better remember me wholly, because your memories are going to live on a lot longer then you are."

"So said Rome," Aegamemnor said.

"The Togas were brilliant, but the Vandals were far less so," Jenny replied.

"Nero fiddled while Rome burned." Aegamemnor rose, the city in inferno.

"Actually," Jenny said from the head of the classroom, pointing at the chalkboard, "that is a myth. He was very concerned about the burning. You really should take notes."

Aegenor slammed her book shut in the front row, and Jenny ran to dodge pages the size of buildings. Luckily, the ink letters were as high as trees, so they prevented her from getting crushed, and she was able to make it to the boats. Aegamemnor, however was going to burn the ships so no one could leave the siege of Troy. That would not do at all, so Jenny had to get her horn out to break down the walls of Jericho. When the walls fell, the siege was done and she could move her wooden horse in—but Aegamemnor was ready for her and it turned out she'd been leading her wooden horse right into the glue factory. That wouldn't do, either. At least she could break it down, because inside of it she had been hiding her spaceship.

"Your spaceship?"

"My story."

Unfortunately the spaceship was crewed by monkeys, but the first animal in space was actually Laika the dog, so the Soviet Union threw them all a Parade on Communist Mars, where Aladdin's father Kalingkata was born.

Aegamemnor stopped. Aladdin's father. This wasn't supposed to go there. This was a wild goose chase.

"Aegenor, listen to me."

"I'm here," she whispered from beneath the misty

surf.

"I want you to remember Aladdin."

"I do."

"I know you've been alone, Aegenor. So very alone."

"I have." The ocean wept.

"But it doesn't have to be that way. I'm going to share something with you, a memory about Aladdin's father."

"No!" Aegamemnor yelled.

"I want to see it."

Memnor twitched at the memory of seeing memories, and Aegamemnor had never been more afraid in her short life. They were waking up. She could feel their dreams coalescing into daylight. She could feel herself beginning to not exist.

"She's dead, Kalingkata. This is done. You don't have to worry about it anymore. Go home, use the fat check I just cut you, and drink some mimosas."

Kalingkata shook his head. "Something is bothering me about this, Hexie. Something she said before she died."

"She was insane. Don't let her deathbed ramblings get into your head. It's over."

Kalingkata nodded, but later he left. He searched out Backgammon Kate's address and hacked the locks. When he entered, he found the place smelled disgusting. He turned the lights on and made his way through the place. She hadn't been dead that long. It shouldn't smell this bad, he thought. But he soon learned the why. There was a crib, and in that crib was a baby. It looked like it hadn't eaten in some time, and it smelled like death and shit. Kalingkata picked up the baby, which was too weak to even cry, and changed its diaper. There were sores all over the baby girl from the exposure, and Kalingkata was revolted by Backgammon Kate. Even if she'd come back right after her attempt to kill you, things wouldn't have been much better for the child. This baby suffered the consequences of her mother's poor choices. He carefully fed the baby formula and took her to the hospital where he faked some identification, paid the bills from Kate's accounts, and then marched straight over to the orphanage.

Kalingkata stood in the cold, artificial snow falling from the roof of the dome to melt on his face and on the heated pavement (engineered to simulate winter without the inconvenience of road crews). In his arms was a tiny baby named Jenny. You'd think him a sap, he thought.

He walked in.

"Are you dropping off a child?" The lady at the desk asked nonchalantly.

"Sort of. How much does this place cost to run?"

"I don't know, I'd have to ask my boss."

"Great. I've set up a trust fund for this child, and another fund which will channel directly to this facility. If you take care of this child, raise her to be smart, independent, well fed and well educated, then every year you will receive enough credits to run this whole facility for a year. Starting with a bonus of that amount today."

The lady was silent for a moment. "Get out of here."

"You don't think I'm serious?" Kalingkata hit some keys on his arm PC. "A gesture of good faith. Check your accounts."

The lady did. She raised her eyebrows.

"I think my boss should come talk to you."

"I think she should."

The meeting went smoothly. Kalingkata filled out some forms and left with a handshake and a threat.

"I'll be checking up on her, and if she isn't happy, I will destroy all of you in ways you have yet to even dream of.

Have a good day!" He walked out, leaving a baby, all his money, and his guilt at the door.

"He really did that for you? Why would he do that?"

"Because he was kind."

Aegenor rose from the surf, naked as she'd never been. "I want to get out of here."

Aegamemnor wailed, fading fast. She had known her own existence so briefly.

Memnor trembled with the memories and tried to flee, running through the void of memory like a lost bird.

Jenny was ready for it.

Aegamemnor was close to being a color that you forgot how to see, a note of music your ears couldn't hear.

"I want to exist.

I want to be Aegenor, whoever that is."

And suddenly there was only Aegenor and Jenny, standing alone in a room of boiling copper, while the Doubling Cube glowed blue with the soul of Memnor. Jenny smiled and pocketed it, then looked down at Aegenor. Pitiful Aegenor, so sure of herself, bleeding out of her face, brought down so low. Jenny pulled her med kit out and began to sterilize the wound, then applied the coagulant to stop the bleeding.

"Thank you," Aegenor muttered.

"Don't thank me, I cut your eye out."

"But you saved me," she whimpered.

Jenny looked away, "It gets worse from here.""

* * * * *

Jenny walked onto the bridge where Aladdin and the Hypercubes had led the Index troops to a resounding victory over the troops on Memnor's ship. She had believed in the kid the whole way. Aladdin was talking to a tall Rimward man.

"Now Maximus, I want the whole ship to blow up, and it needs to look like an accident. An accident that happens after we get out of shooting range."

"Why an accident?"

"So when we get out of shooting range no one wants to follow us too badly." Maximus shrugged.

"Whatever you want, boss."

"That's my man!" Jenny was proud. Aladdin was growing into quite the young man. He looked over and waved at her as she retracted the wheels on her rollerblades so they became boots, and clomped over. "I see you got the ship in order."

"It won't be in order for long. We're blowing it up."

"Smart plan. Did you raid the computer systems?" Aladdin gave her the most condescending look a beaten and tortured young man who still hadn't located his shirt could manage.

"Jenny, really, who do you think I am?"

"Alright, alright, you raided their computers."

"How did you get on here anyway?"

"Does it matter?"

He leaned on the console. "It might."

"Stowed away in the Index shuttle that offloaded your little troupe here." She gestured with her katana at the Index troops, who were looting the ship with the glee of people who were aware the vessel they were pillaging was going to become a firecracker fairly soon.

"Speaking of which, I have a favor to ask of you, Aladdin. I need you to drop me off on the Honor of the Outcast on the way back. I need to give your dad something that Hex shouldn't get her hands on." She spoke not in English, but in the code language the Spinneret used. Aladdin had figured it out at an early age.

"I don't know what you just said," he said in English. "But it won't be a problem, I'll drop you off." He finished in code.

Jenny nodded. Good boy. She started walking off, but she realized there was someone right behind her.

"What you want, Anya?"

"I just wanted to tell you that I really admire you, and I wish I could go around having adventures like you do. I dream of that."

Jenny kept walking. "You'll get your chance, Anya, and then you'll wish you never dreamed of it."

* * * * *

Aladdin sat in your foyer. He was wearing a new suit, since the old one had exploded (aside from the pants, which had been ripped up and dirtied beyond reasonable use anyway).

He hadn't been out on many missions on this internship. He mainly made your coffee and managed your schedule, but the last few days had been quite the adventure.

He thought of Aegenor. He hadn't gotten along with her, but she was a good person and deserved better than what had happened to her. At least Jenny had killed her so she didn't become like Jade. It was...horrible to think that though. Deep down he wished she'd survived. Depite everything.

He thought of the Hypercubes, of Anya, whom he hoped would be forever better than her mother. On their parting, he had told her to her face that he had no idea who her mother was. Of course he knew, it was obvious, but he couldn't tell her. She deserved better than that. She deserved the mother she dreamed about. Ulysses deserved the father he dreamed of too, but Aladdin had no idea who that was.

Aladdin thought of Nightingale, whom he missed, whom he couldn't wait to see again, who had fought so hard her whole life. If only Aladdin could live up to that level of commitment, that level of devotion.

Of course he could, he realized. It was to her, and the dream of her dreams coming true. Aladdin looked up at the Picasso painting you had casually hung in your foyer; Nightingale would never be able to afford that.

That was when Aladdin realized his life really was defined by the women around him. He latched onto them, he fought for them, he called on them for strength...but what did Jhe Aladdin want? When the story was told, what would his place be in it? Would he be the hero? Or would he be the sidekick? Would he be on the side of the winners, supporting the Anyas who dreamed of adventure, the Nightingales who dreamed of freedom, the Jennys who dreamed of independence?

Yes. Yes he would. And he'd be okay with that. He didn't have to be the hero, he just had to be happy. That was the moment Aladdin realized that being a man didn't mean being in charge of the world or others, it meant being in charge of yourself.

"Aladdin dear, could you come in? I've heard you had quite the adventure."

Aladdin unbuttoned his top button and loosened his tie. In charge of himself, indeed.

"Chess Mistress Hex, you have no idea the kind of game I've been playing. It would make less sense to you then Red Breaker chess."

* * * * *

Anya Hypercube sat in the living room and watched Valentinez march his toy horse along the floor. It didn't feel the same. She'd been back for a few days now, and nothing felt the same. When her family ate dinner, what had been the most joyous communion of unity felt hollow compared to her time in the stars. She went out at night and stared at the sky in the spot she had sat with Aladdin. The stars were so vast, and her mother was out there somewhere, as was Ulysses dad. She did some searching and found that Geraldine had once lived on Mars for a while. That was all she needed to know. It didn't take her long to decide she was going to run away from home and go adventuring.

"Want to play a game Anya?"

Anya shrugged. "Sure, Valentinez. Why not? What game?"

"I dunno."

She sighed, and ran through games in her head. "Backgammon?" Oddly fitting, she thought, smirking to herself.

"Sure!"

Anya reached into her pocket and pulled out the parting gift Jenny had given her. "You're in luck. While I was gone, I got a special tool for the game!"

Valentinez looked at the cube warily. It glowed blue, almost supernaturally. "What is it?"

"It's just a doubling cube silly, now let's play." She set the cube down to "2" and set the board.

Inside the cube, Memnor screamed silently, eternally, and hopelessly. Later, he was put away into the game cabinet, and no one ever knew he should be God.

FILE 18:
THE GOOD SIN

Carnival Reichenbach was formed by a group of misfits on Ceres station in the late 2400s. They had been poor and on the streets, and sold their own blood to buy their instruments. They began as a cover band, performing a lot of religious rock music (Bowie, Elvis, Beyonce), but eventually they began writing their own tunes. Once they had a few hits, they catapulted to success as one of the few bands to tour both Earth and Mars. Their music is found in the ears of many a teenager, and in the ears of Backgammon Jenny. They wrote songs about love, about violence, about freedom. Jenny liked all those things. Aegenor had only known the second one.

Aegenor had been in a box a long time, drugged. She didn't know that, though, when she woke up chained in a cell. Voices drifted into her awareness, and she realized she wasn't alone.

"She's awake. Took her long enough. You drugged her too much."

"I was in the field, it's hard to judge there."

Aegenor's vision wasn't the same. With only one eye, her depth perception was all messed up, but she could see Backgammon Jenny, and...an alien? Where was she?

Jenny walked over and looked her in the eye. "I want you to know that I'm sorry for what I'm about to do. I'm so very sorry."

Aegenor shook. "Please, just let me go. I'm sorry."

"You have memories we need, and there is only one person who can get them out of you. Are you ready?"

Aegenor heard a voice in her head, a voice she could somehow tell Jenny could hear, too. "Oh, I'm very ready. Thank you, Jenny. I'm so very grateful for your loyalty to Kalingkata!"

Jenny looked away and, shuddering, walked out of the room with a parting, "Just get the information we need for the war, Jade. I don't want anything more to do with this."

"Hello, Aegenor. You're Aladdin's friend, right? We're going to have a lot of fun together. I'm his mommy. And I'm not going to lie, this is going to hurt a lot, Aegenor."

"What do you want from me?"

"The plans of the Council's fleet. You have the memories of one of the Council's members, who is now deceased of course, but those memories are very valuable to us here. And to me especially."

"You're a ghost? Like Aladdin said..."

"No, Aegenor, you should be bowing. I'm not just a ghost. I control your life and death, so from this moment on, I'm your God."

Aegenor strained at her chains. There was no way to break them.

"You like struggling. That's good." The sadism in Jade Darkshadow's voice was thick as infected butter. "You don't control me. I'm me."

"You poor naive fool. Nothing that's yours isn't mine now. And you'll be my ticket to power. I'll crush The Emperors' fleet, and I'll enjoy every moment of it."

Aegenor screamed for help, but no help came. Then Jade pushed herself into the deepest recesses of Aegenor's mind, and the screams and tears didn't stop for hours.

It didn't take that long for Jade to get the information she needed for the war, she was just having so much goddamn fun. And Jade knew that Jenny could hear every one of the screams from outside the door.

After a while, Jenny reached into her coat with shaking hands and put her headphones on. She jacked up the Carnival Reichenbach until she could barely hear the screams and listened to songs about freedom to cover up the agony of the freedom she'd destroyed.

This was what Backgammon Jenny did. She made the Devil's bargains the saints couldn't for the sake of Heaven. It was, wasn't it? This was the right thing?

Aegenor's scream cut through the music, and Jenny tried to turn it up, but it wouldn't go any louder.

Some things she would just have to live with.

* * * * *

"So that's it." Aegenor said, curled against the wall of the cell, spooning through her mushy prison rations. It had taken bribes of the kind I never thought I would have to give to get this interview, but I needed to know the rest of the story. She'd been very helpful, especially since she had so many people's memories in her head. She was a sad girl, and understandably so. I think if she could kill herself, she would have, but she was too valuable an informant for them to let that happen. So here she was in a cell on the Honor of the Outcast.

"So, this story about Jhe Aladdin. It's really about Backgammon Jenny in the end...weird," I mused.

Her one eye turned toward me. "You missed the whole point of the story, Mr. Fredrickson. This story isn't about one person. It's about the people who pull the strings. about Jade Darkshadow. It's about how she stole a boy and tried to make him into a weapon and failed, about how she abandoned a daughter who rose above anything her mother ever did, how she hurt me...And it's about Memnor who thought it could be everyone's master, and became noones, and it's most of all about Chess Mistress Hex and how she corrupted Kalingkata's most trusted lieutenant, and how she destroyed me, and destroyed so much...and is only going to destroy more."

I stopped writing.

"What do you mean, 'destroy more'?"

"I mean this war is going to be over soon." She stared into me, her eye like Odin's. "And we're all going to wish we'd made a higher wager at the start of it."

The ship rocked with a hit from some far off weapon, and she stared at me until I left. The only Aegenor, alone, like she had always been, cast away from the starlight.

FILE 19:
ALL BETS ARE UP, THE DEALER IS ALL IN

You were there, Chess Mistress Hex, and your decisions made this happen. I can only guess why you decided to take the exact path you did here, but that's not my job. I have seen the videos, and I can take a guess. What happened next, though, that was all you. You asked me to tell you, so I will oblige.

There you were, at the head of that big table. Your face was a perfect mask, neither smiling nor stern. Unreadable. You sipped your tea perfectly. You had all the important people there, but somehow only the important people who wouldn't say no. What a stroke of luck, what a great and fortuitous moment. There was Aequitas, fearsome as ever. There was Jade, a bubbling cube of monstrosity and body horror. There was Backgammon Jenny, goggles over her eyes as though she was trying to hide herself from you. She probably was. Was that a twitch of a smile on your face? No, no you're too good for that.

"To business then."

"Where's everyone else?" Jenny asked, a tiny tremble in her voice. I know you picked up on it, but no one else did.

"Now now, Jenny, we have everyone we need. The decision has already been made. We're the ones who have taken the brunt of this war. This long and piteous, unprofitable war. It's time for us to end it, in one swift stroke that will establish the Rim once and for all as the real power in the Solar System. Aequitas and I have no need of lesser beings to make decisions for us."

"You presume a lot of yourself," he growled at you.

You actually smiled. "Of course, dear. I say too much. You have the codes, Jenny?"

She nodded and gave some spiel about them, explaining the documents as she handed them over.

You kept smiling. You didn't stop. "I'm sure our friend Jade here can do quite a lot with this, can't you Jade?"

The box quivered. I don't really know what it was thinking, because it was an undead abomination against nature, but it certainly thought something.

"Wonderful. Then the plan can go into effect. We've arranged for a strike team to to infiltrate the Council's ships, and using this information, we should be able to take control of the ships of the fleet. What a pity, having an empire of so many races you can't trust. It makes you take steps that are ever so exploitable."

Jenny's hand shook a bit under the table.

"We're going to eradicate them, every single threat, and then, at long last, we shall have peace."

"My people will be the ones to make the cut. You couldn't pull the blade across their skin if you tried," Aequitas said.

You smiled. Who knows if he was right, but either way, you never have to do the dirty work.

"Of course, Aequitas. That's why this is an alliance. If I could do this all by myself, I would."

I can't read Citlal biology, so I really don't know what the reaction meant. It was a weird dark humming underscored with a low thumping beat.

I do know how to read Jenny's reaction. The tremble in her hands. The doubt in her eyes.

The twinkle in yours.

An elite commando unit, or maybe a ragtag band of rapscallions, reports vary, infiltrated the Council fleet. Codes were input. Computer systems were routed by code and edits. The failsafes sound so terrible in hindsight: so many species from so many alternate realities and worlds all shoved into one armada. If one got uppity, there had to be a way to kill them. Having such a failsafe was dangerous though, so the Council spared no expense in building it. The system was so safe, so secure. Memnor's security experts had worked for longer than many beings live to build this system, so foolproof, so difficult to trick. So difficult in fact, you'd need the head of the Council's Intelligence Bureau to get around it, and oh what a lucky girl you are, Mistress Hex, because you placed your bets that you could get exactly that.

And oh you did. Turn the cube to 64. Cash in.

It was over in minutes. I wish I could describe it grandly for you, but there was nothing grand about it. One moment, there was a fleet. The next moment, trickles of dots floated out of the massive, motionless ships. They were so small, and any dramatization would have to increase the scale to ridiculous proportions to make a visual impression.

Despite its blandness, this was a moment of death unimaginable.

No fanfare, no explosions, just corpses.

What face did you make then, I wonder, staring off into the stars? You could say every soldier in the council was a war criminal, but I suppose you could say that about us now, too. They floated off, and the specks blotted out only a smattering of the stars.

They were dead, and the universe spun on.

The Council's fleet was wiped out, but The Emperors of the Great Assimilation had their own fleet, so there was still much to be done. You won half a war, and won it brilliantly and bloodily. It was a conclusion to a plan, but not the whole story. This was just a moment in the conflict, a blink in its horror, malice, and shining wonder.

Of course, the ships were all claimed by Aequitas. He pulled the knife, and grabbed the man's wallet as he fell.

It's funny, though. You didn't mind killing all those people, but you made sure Aladdin wasn't there to see it. Here we are at the end, and I can't even write in our protagonist.

What's a writer to do?

Cut ahead, I suppose.

Aladdin walked through the halls of the Honor of the Outcast. He'd learned what happened. He wasn't there, but he knew finally. He knows he retrieved that data, and he knows that even in his ignorance, he was responsible for a mass killing. He's not an idiot. Sure, he doesn't know the details, but he has a general picture. He saw Jenny in the hallway. She stepped out of a door. He looked at her. She didn't meet his gaze.

"It's a war, Aladdin. We saved a lot of lives by doing this. A lot of lives," she said.

"Thus spake the bombers over Hiroshima," he replied.

He turns and puts his hands in his pockets. He walks.

There has been death. He lost Andromeda...he thought he'd lost Aegenor, too.

What a change to lose a friend to something other than death. To see her in the reflection of the glass in front of you as you walk away, lip quivering, uncertain of how to fix what's been broken. All bets were in, doubling cube up to 64, but what good is winning a game when your friends won't return to the table?

Unknown to him, a few decks below, Aegenor shivered in the endless pinpricks of light.

Life goes on. Somewhere, at least. Maybe not here.

FILE 20:
EPILOGUE: EDITS

You turn the pages of this report, and I watch your face closely during the entire time you read the manuscript. Your assistant Alexis brings you tea. At the end of our meeting, you asked me to add this on to the end, so here we are. You finish reading. I wait for your verdict.

"It's...adequate.."

"Thanks, I think."

"I mean, darling, that there are some real problems here. I still don't really see the need for the chess games...but that's your artistic license and I can respect that." You smiled a smile that was charming, indulgent, and utterly false.

I thought of trying to explain again, but decided against it.

"I do think you should cut out the whole part where Aladdin and Nightingale go into that haunted house spacestation in the bubble dimension on Aequitas' orders. You already have one example of them having an adventure together, two seems superfluous. Plus it doesn't really relate to the plot."

She had me there. "Yes Mistress Hex, I'll cut it."

"Good, good. There are also some moments where you portray me in a less than flattering light. I'm surprised, Carl. That's a bolder move than I'd have expected of you."

Part of me wanted to apologize, the other half wanted to say something witty and self-asserting. Instead I said, "Oh."

"But overall I enjoyed it. What did you think?" She wasn't looking at me, but at a woman in the corner of the room. She wore a long brown coat with a half moon, half sun symbol on the back and left breast. Her head was shaved on the left side from the temple down, with her blonde hair combed to the other side. She wore white pants, practical boots, and a gray turtleneck. She was skinny, a thin beanpole frame layered in tight, thick muscle.

"He could have gone further," the woman said in a slurred monotone, "gotten a little more sick with you. Not that I'm complaining." She grabbed a chair, an antique 23rd century Italian model, and swung it over towards your desk, sitting down and putting her feet up in one lithe motion. You smiled politely, but I could tell you didn't appreciate her feet on the desk. Her facial expression didn't change once during our conversation, her voice never left its monotone.

"Carl Fredrickson, I don't believe you've ever had the pleasure. Meet Kinan Jans. She also has a vested interest in the Council's destruction."

"I also have a vested interest in my friends. You manipulated my friend Jenny."

"And you let me."

"I encouraged her. We're not all as dumb as you think."

"Excuse me," I cut in, "how did she get in here?"

"Oh, darling,," you put your hand on mine like you were reassuring a toddler, "hush."

Kinan sits down, and crosses her legs, putting her feet up on the coffee table.

"It's not a bad story though. Tragic though. You must feel so safe working here away from the bloodshed. Aladdin and Aegenor were teenagers."

"You're getting far too sentimental," you say

Kinan looks at me, "So is this really your ending? Are you okay with this?"

"I don't know you, honestly."

"You leave a broken boy thinking his friend is dead, and leave her maimed in a dungeon. You clearly have the moral high ground here."

I sputter, "I'm just writing this down!"

Kinan leans in, you watch her curious, "Then change the ending so it's worth writing about."

"I can't get her out of that dungeon, I don't have the clout."

"You have the knowledge, and you know people who can."

I look at you. You're bemused, playing with your teacup.

"So c'mon then Carl, you've been told who this story was about over and over. But who's telling the damn thing?"

I stand up. I start walking. That turns into an awkward hustle. Then a jog. I hear you behind me, laughing. I need to find Aladdin. I need to get Aegenor out of that hole of darkness. I'll even buy her a new eye, hell.

I have calls to make. Things to figure out. I can't just observe this anymore.

It's time to take a stand.

Even if I wouldn't bet on me.

/File End

Miss Librarian,

The following two Appendixes have been provided to allow you some greater insight into the lives of the Hypercube family, especially the "twins" Anya and Ulysses, as well as one event following the course of this report.

-Carl

APPENDIX 1:
THE MOTHER'S DAY MACHINE

"Okay." Anya said, "I think it's ready to go."

Ulysses looked at the rejiggered, duck taped, and overall messy contraption Anya had whipped together. "I thought I remembered what this was supposed to do Anya, but I have to be honest, I have lost all semblance of knowing what that thing even is anymore."

Anya wiped the sweat off her brow and smiled back at him, as something whirred briefly inside the machine, even though it was turned off. "It's Geraldine's Mother's day present."

"I know it's that, but what actually is it?" Anya stared at it a moment, as if she too had forgotten in her own excitement, "It's an old plastic molder. You can pop programs of 3D objects into it, and the right materials, and it bakes you up plastic stuff. Geraldine is always complainin' about losing little things with all the kids around the house, so I figure giving her a mini-factory should do the trick."

"Did you get this out of a junk yard?"

"You carried it out of the junk yard."

Ulysses recalled the trip to the junkyard, but not carrying this machine... "How many things did you put together to make this?"

"A few."

"Does it work?"

"I haven't tried it yet."

"You *are* testing this before you give this to mom."

"Fine. But what did you get her?"

"A necklace, it matches her cybernetic limbs and eye."

Anya smiled, "That will be cute on her."

"Well I hope so." He took a deep breath, "so what do you want to try to make first? Something simple."

"A spoon."

"There is no spoon."

"It can make a spoon! I promi-"

"It was a reference."

She nodded, "Of course." Anya bit her tongue, and touched a few buttons, the machine whirred, and smoke belched out of it... But it produced one perfectly formed plastic spoon.

"Happy Mother's day to my step-mom."

Ulysses smirked, "To my mom."

Mother's Day came, and the whole family was there, one by one, the gifts were given. The younger kids mainly gave handmade things, that Geraldine fawned over like the precious and adorable pieces of unusable effort they were, and the older kids gave more practical things she'd been wanting. Ulysses gave his necklace, which his mother was jubilant at seeing, and kissed her tall son on the cheek, pulling his head down by the hair to do so. Anya waited till last, and unveiled her contraption. It didn't look like much, but it made things out of plastic alright.

"Could it make me a teacup?"

Anya was grinning more than her face could quite take, "Of course!" The machine whirred, out popped a teacup. "A teapot?" Out came that to. Geraldine was veritably beaming at Anya, and Ulysses watched as they began a lively discussion about programming the machine to produce stylized casings for their robotic limbs. Ulysses had expected the machine to break, to be honest. He'd expected to have to pull Anya out of another tough situation, like that horrible night he'd dragged her from the crashed speeder. But there she was, triumphant.

And even though his own mom was ignoring his necklace to talk to Anya and the glory of her gizmo, that was fine. He didn't know who his father was, and Anya didn't know who her mom was. Their whole lives Anya made a point of calling Geraldine by her name rather than any term of endearment, even though they got along great, but this Mother's Day was worth it for him just to hear Anya slip and call Geraldine, just once, in the middle of a sentence, mom. Geraldine didn't even notice, at least as far as Ulysses could tell. But it made Ulysses feel like their family was whole, that no one was missing, that despite his clearly different paternity he was Michelangelo's son, and Anya Geraldine's daughter.

But that was what made their family, he thought, Anya didn't have to call Geraldine mom for her to love her. Nor be her blood.

But that didn't mean that Ulysses wouldn't enjoy the moment.

APPENDIX 2:
THE EXCESS SON

Ulysses looked like a brute. When he walked down the street, people gave him space. When he went to work out, some girls were scared of him, and some flocked to him like he was a demigod. But none of them really got that he wasn't just a pile of muscle. Outside of his family, he was an outsider, a locked room which he peered keenly out of from his auburn eyes. He was a titan, he could crush a man's forearm no problem, no effort. But he was Ulysses at heart, and he saw the world like an odyssey. He went to pick up his dad's dry cleaning, and noticed the tell tale twitches of the man behind the counter. He smoothed his words to get a discount. The fact that he looked like he could smash people's skulls in always made them underestimate him. Always made them misjudge him. Put them off guard. And it was their luck he didn't give a damn about manipulating them for anything more than discounts.

Because when it came down to it, Ulysses was a family man. Hopefully one of his own someday, if he ever found a woman who could actually comprehend who he was that he wasn't related to, and for now, the family he had. His parents, his brothers and sisters, and Anya, who while not actually related to him, was the closest he was to anyone. She was like his twin, and she was only a tiny bit older then him so it was close enough. Children from previous relationships, with twelve siblings, best of friends.

This isn't about Anya though, she left a few days ago, to go find the parents of both of them who had apparently abandoned them, and Ulysses' parents were out trying to negotiate new treaties, so Ulysses was a glorified babysitter. Glorified, but necessary, after that weird alien had tried to kill off his family.

"Ule! ULE!" He looked up, Eowyn was standing there, holding Murasaki in a very loose headlock.

"Oh, Eowyn, not again."

"I have conquered my sister!"

"Yes, I can see that."

"Get off of me!"

"Eowyn let go of your sister."

"But I won."

Ulysses gave her a look, a stern look, but not a cold one. It was a look carefully crafted over decades of having over a dozen siblings. She let go. "Good girl. Now, how about you two go get yourself a snack?"

"Will you help us make it? I want apples."

"I want celery."

"I wand celery and apples."

"You kids are freaks." He got up, chuckling to himself, and soon found himself slicing up apples and celery and getting peanut butter in cups to dip them in. He sliced the sticks just right for the size of his sister's hands. He did the math about how much peanut butter they'd need. They devoured it, and began running around again: another satisfied loved one. That was when Ulysses heard the buzzer go off for the gate, checked the monitor, saw the man standing there, and the day got a whole lot less simple. Ulysses didn't think this would be very impressive trip. People came to the gates all the time, for business, because they had the wrong address, because one of Zoro's ex boy or girlfriends really wanted him back, it could be any number of things. Once Hypatia even had some guy with a crush on her drop off a love poem. He'd been surprised that anyone had noticed her, with all those books in between her and other people's eyes, but it had made him happy to see her read the badly written poem, all a giggle.

This wasn't that kind of day. At the gate was a man, from Earth by the looks of him, mid thirties. He had a little girl with him, who looked terrified as hell, like she had stepped from Earth onto a moon made up entirely of pirates who cut their limbs off and replaced them with robot parts just for fun. He gave her a smile. She smiled back. At least Ulysses knew he was good at something.

"Welcome to the Hypercube residence. What business do you have with the Cube2Hypergang, or the Hypercube family?" The man, who was dirty as a dust storm, and his clothes ripped enough to be fashionable with the right crowd, sheepishly smiled.

"Is this... Is Geraldine McGraw Hypercube here?"

"My mom? What business do you have with her."

"I... I'd rather talk to her about that in person." The child, who was clinging to the man's pant leg as though she were in the ocean, and he was her life preserver stared into Ulysses eyes. She looked familiar somehow.

"I'm afraid I can't let you in unless I know the nature

of your business sir. Family rules." The man bit his lip, and stuttered for a bit. Ulysses stared back coolly.

"I.... I think she's my mother."

Ulysses could have stared forever. In that man, and his daughter, he saw the tell tale signs of his mother's genetics. The little traits she'd passed on to himself and all of his non-Anya siblings. The cheekbones. The eyes. The wrists that bulged a tiny bit where they connected to the hand.

"I think you should come in. And I think we need to talk in private."

The man sat in the wing chair in the dirty parlor, mom had meant to clean it a year ago. She kept not getting around to it. The man's daughter was playing with Eowyn and Murasaki, and the three seemed to be getting along well enough that they weren't being interrupted yet, so no complaints.

"Myself and my daughter got off Earth right after the blockade ended.... My wife didn't make it... She got..." he trailed off, and stared out the window. Ulysses let the man take his time. He wasn't having an easy time. "My name is Gerald Martinow."

"Ulysses Hypercube."

"It's good to meet you... So I expect you want to know my story."

"You'd be right. I'm listening. I'm patient. You want anything to drink?" The man shook his head, "any food?" Ulysses should have thought of that himself. He commed Leonidas, "Leo, get me some sandwiches in here stat."

"You aren't a doctor, man," he grumbled back,

"Yeah, and you're a deli worker as of now. Bring some chips and a drink to." Leo just sighed. Ulysses had won, of course.

"Continue, please." The man unbuttoned his top button on his shirt, and loosened his tie. Judging by the circles under his eyes, he hadn't had a full night's rest in days.

"My father was a Centro banker, not high enough up that he was making important decisions, but high enough he was wealthy. My mother was a painter, not the artistic kind, the outside of houses and such. Though, I think she wanted to be an artist... Anyways, she always hated me. I had other siblings, ones I don't really know if are alive or dead right now..."

"I'm sorry."

He nodded, "It's... The way of things now isn't it? Wars come and rip our families apart, split us up from the people we care about the most..."

"I know the feeling somewhat right now."

"I'm sorry to hear that. Well, look, I don't know how to say this, but I always suspected that I wasn't my mother's child. I didn't look like her, or act like her, and she always looked at me like I was some sort of..."

"Betrayal."

"Yeah, that's the word... And I found I didn't have a birth record from Earth when I started looking into it. It was from Rimward space. No mother listed."

"I see. Can I see your documents?" The man seemed startled, as though Ulysses was going to turn him over to the authorities. Then the man remembered he was in Rimward space, and pulled out a datapad. Ulysses skimmed through the Documents.

"Well, I'm afraid you can't be my mother's son, Mister Martinow. She would have been twelve when she had you, if this is correct."

"It is correct."

"Then I think any further discussion would waste both

of our times, I have a lot to do." Leo entered with a finely crafted tray of sandwiches, and the look on his face said, "I heard your last sentence, and I cannot have made all these for nothing."

"You and your daughter can of course eat before you leave."

"I'm not done... There's more."

"More about what?" Leo said, setting the tray down.

"Leave the room Leo, we're discussing something very important." Ulysses held his look. He was getting better and better at holding that look.

"Fine, whatever." The door slammed behind Leo, and Ulysses turned back to Mister Martinow, his shirt bending with the contours of his muscles like some sort of high powered machine moving under a sheet.

"After I got off Earth, I started looking, to see if I could find more about my family here... I didn't find anything in the hospitals... So I started tracking down back alley Doctors."

"That's pretty damn dangerous, sir."

"It was."

"You could have endangered your daughter."

"I never took her with me!"

"You could have endangered your daughter." The gaze was turned on, and Martinow slinked back a bit in his chair.

"In... Indeed I could have. I'm sorry." He said, not sure even why he just apologized.

"Continue, please."

"Yes, well, I started finding records of... Child prostitution rings."

Ulysses stood up, his eyes were like a curdling sun. "If you're insinuating my family would ever even consider running a-"

"No! I'm saying your parents were both children in one!"

There was a silence as deafening as the deep space only miles above their heads. "What did you say?"

"I'm saying that the records seem to indicate that your mother and father, and the other founding members of Cube2Hypergang were… Child prostitutes who killed their enslavers."

"I don't believe you. That's ridiculous. Get the hell out of my house." The man simply held out a datapad, and Ulysses stared at It, then grabbed it furiously. He scrolled through the data. And then he scrolled through it again. And again. And again. And then he threw it on the floor. The man stared, waiting for a response.

"I'll put you up in a hotel for the night. I need to think about this."

"And… You read about me in there? That I'm her kid from…"

"From being raped by your asshole of a father when she was eleven. Yeah. I read it. You'll have a warm place to stay tonight. Now get the hell out of my house." The man nodded, and Leo escorted him and his daughter to the gate, and gave them a data card for housing credit. Ulysses shut off the monitor he watched that on, and slumped down in his chair. Anya and him were both learning things about their parents. He just hoped what she was learning were things she actually wanted to know.

Ulysses didn't really sleep that night. He stared, which was usual for him, but only at the ceiling. He would have cried, if he hadn't gotten so used to not crying for the sake of all of his siblings. Any one of them could barge in needing him, at any time. He couldn't risk tears. But he wanted to weep. "Mom…" he muttered, "How could anyone do that to you..." he wasn't going to cry. He couldn't risk it.

He rolled over. These weren't tears in his eyes, his body was just expelling salty liquid.

He wasn't crying... And he definitely wasn't weeping.

Ulysses showed up at the hotel around lunchtime. Zoro and Denise, which was the worst name for a long term girlfriend ever, had agreed to watch the house while he was away. He rung the doorbell. No response. He knocked. No response. He knocked harder, and the door cracked open a tad. The little girl looked at him, her whole body was trembling slightly.

"Daddy says to come back another time..."

"Are you okay? What's wrong?" He squatted down to eye level with her.

"Nothings wrong. You can't come in."

"I paid for the hotel, doesn't that mean I can?"

She shook her head slowly. Like a doll. Like.... Ulysses felt sick. He didn't have to think very long to decide to ram the door in. The girl might break some bones, but that would be better than the alternative. His shoulder was like an oxen, and the door hairline fractured as he rammed it. The girl was shoved backwards... But not as backwards as she should have been, because a long segmented tendril covered in thin spines was dug into her spine, and she lifted up from the ground a bit as the tendril tried to save its puppet. Ulysses didn't stop moving. He didn't stop looking. There was her father, sitting on the bed, glassy eyed, another tendril dug into his spine. Ulysses was angry now. He hated mister Martinow, a bit, for no fault of that man's own, but he couldn't blame a child. And he couldn't let anything do that to a person.

Ulysses didn't dodge the first tendril that shot at him, he just grabbed it, and began wrestling the armored muscular thing to the ground. It writhed, and he bent it too far, and there was a snap. Electricity and ooze seeped from the wound, and it thrashed even more violently, slicing up Ulysses' forearms. Ulysses tried to barrel forward, but the thing put the child in front of him, her face smiling back at him like a baby doll. "You deserve this for killing my family Ulysses Hypercube."

"Yours tried to kill mine!"

"Yours deserved to die."

He could tell that reasoning with this thing was going to work wonders. Luckily, Ulysses was always staring, and he caught in the open air the momentary glimpse of a finger over a mouth, and another finger pointing towards the north wall. Ulysses didn't question. This was too dangerous for questions. Lives were on the line. He edged north.

"I'll break your bones, and kill your little siblings off one by one. I'll start with the other one you came with, with the metal limbs." Ulysses was definitely not mentioning she wasn't around for that.

"Try it." It swung at him, using the bodies it had on its tendrils like clubs. Ulysses gritted his teeth. He knew what the right thing to do was. He did it. When the tendrils came towards him, he rammed into the base, below where the bodies were attached. The spines sprung out, and dug deep into his flesh, and he could see his own blood pooling on the floor. But the father and daughter weren't smashed to bits. He would have breathed a sigh of relief, if the thing hadn't started constricting around him, like a python made of knives. He struggled against it, threw his weight back and forth, but he was losing a lot of blood, and this thing was giving it it's all.

This made it all the better for Jhe Aladdin, who had been tailing Ulysses on the way to the hotel, hidden beneath a chameleon cloak, to set off the triggered burn gel he had been applying to the spots between the creature's plates. It would have screamed, but it simply thrashed, and the last thing Ulysses saw before he passed out was Aladdin drop the cloak to the ground, pull a gun out of his shirt, and fire come streaming out of it onto the already burning creature.

Hypatia was the first person he saw when he awoke. She was looking over him, her face a scrunchy of worry, that lit up with delight when he opened his eyes. "You're alive!"

"I'm awake."

"They go together stupid." She hugged him. The hug hurt a lot.

He laughed. "Good to see you to."

"And you, Ulysses."

There was Aladdin, standing in the corner, circles under his eyes. He'd drawn some sort of design over his face, like a lightning bolt.

"Aladdin, I've never been so happy to see you man, you saved my life."

He nodded, "Before you ask, the father and daughter are okay. The doctors were able to remove the spines from their nervous system without permanent damage. If I'm alive then, I'll tell my father building a Darkshadow hospital here worked out well." There was that Darkshadow name again. Maybe that Darkshadow lady was a doctor? Ulysses didn't know.

"Also, it's good to see you to, Hypatia." Aladdin added, as though he had suddenly realized she was in the room."

"Are you okay man?" Aladdin shrugged.

"Absolutely not. I have a lot of... Things to do."

"You know I'll do anything I can to help."

"Where's your sister? I was hoping to talk to her." Ulysses glanced at his younger sister, "she's... Getting her leg replaced. The one she got malfunctioned, and calling the guys who sold it didn't work out, so she went in person."

Hypatia looked convinced. Aladdin looked like he knew Ulysses was lying, but didn't really give a shit.

"Whatever. Look, she comes by, tell her to call me or something. Oh, and..." His eyes glazed over for a moment. "Oh yes, there's one other thing, I need to tell you about someone, both of you." Aladdin's face got more flush, his eyes more human, "Have you ever heard of the Nightingale, Alice MacLeod? A woman who never would let her family suffer if she could do anything about it..."

Gerald hadn't ever wanted to find out who his mom was, but now he knew. His spine hurt, and the last few weeks were all a blur from when that thing had turned him and his daughter into puppets... He sat in the hospital bed, and pondered the future. He didn't have a home on Earth to go to. He didn't have a friend left living. And then Ulysses entered the room, and he couldn't help but look away.

"Hello, how are you feeling?" the half Korean man said.

"I'm... Sorry. I didn't mean to put you or your family in danger... I was..."

"Mind controlled, yeah, I've seen it before, it ain't pretty. And neither is how you came into this world."

"I'm sorry, I didn't want to find you, my father told me the truth, before he died... I couldn't stand it, I could never look him in the eyes again..."

"And you aren't him. And you are never ever going to tell my mother or father who you are, do you understand?" Ulysses stared. Gerald nodded.

"But, we have dozens of bedrooms in our house that ain't used, and you're my blood. So you and your daughter are living with us now. No arguments. No Hypercube is living on the streets ever again. You two get well, and you're getting a roof and some food. But you betray my trust, and we'll have problems, do you understand me?"

"I... thank you... I.... I don't deserve this. Thank you." Gerald began to cry. Ulysses, stared, not out of any way he could change people's minds by staring... But because he was jealous as hell that Gerald could be crying.

"You're blood. We look after our own. Always. Even when they screw up, or come from parents our parents hate, like I assume my dad and my older sis's mom are hated by my parents. Doesn't matter. You're a Hypercube. You'll be cared for."

Gerald nodded, "Mary will have some friends her own age to then... That's... More than I could ever ask."

Ulysses headed for the door, "you didn't ask, and you'll never have to. That's family. See you when you're better." Ulysses walked out the door, got to a cab, went home, and spent the evening carrying Boudica around on his shoulders while she shouted something about Revolution. "Revolution Boudica? You been reading about your namesake?"

"I'm not Boudica, I'm the Nightingale!"

Ulysses smirked, "You know, I heard some stories about her, would you want to hear em?"

"Yes! Of course I want storytime about Nightingale!"

Valentinez leaned his head out a door, "storytime?" this continued, till the whole family was assembled, even Denise, if she counted, and someone had prepared an impromptu meal people were snacking on. Storytime always ended up this way: an hour to get ready and set up, and it would go all night. This is why he loved his family.

"So," Ulysses started, "You remember our friend Aladdin?"
Everyone nodded, or said yes, except for Valintinez who was being contrary for no reason.

"I'm going to tell you a story about him, and about a girl named Nightingale, and about some things we should treasure. Our freedom, and our family. It all started, when Nightingale's family went hungry...."

ABOUT THE AUTHOR

Carl Fredrickson was born on Oberon, and went to school at Carthage University on its sister moon of Titania, where he graduated with dual degrees in communications and journalism. Carl splits his time between Europa and Ceres these days, but enjoys the occasional vacation to the resorts on Titan.

Carl is a big fan of pasta, chicken tikka masala, and chocolate cake.

You can find more about him easily since you have so much power over his life and death.

ABOUT THE AUTHOR

James Wylder was born in Elkhart Indiana, where he later taught at the High School he graduated from for a time. He now lives in Indianapolis with his girlfriend where he spends a lot of time at the library writing and trying to make his way to lots of restaurants.

James is a big fan of Chinese Buffets, sit-down Mexican restaurants, and any spicy food that doesn't have cilantro in it. He also likes chocolate cake.

You can find out more about him at jameswylder.com.

Made in the USA
San Bernardino, CA
01 September 2017